DOUBLE HONEYMOON

Also by Evan S. Connell

THE ANATOMY LESSON AND OTHER STORIES

MRS. BRIDGE

THE PATRIOT

NOTES FROM A BOTTLE FOUND ON THE BEACH AT CARMEL

AT THE CROSSROADS

THE DIARY OF A RAPIST

MR. BRIDGE

POINTS FOR A COMPASS ROSE

THE CONNOISSEUR

DOUBLE HONEYMOON

EVAN S. CONNELL

COUNTERPOINT
BERKELEY

Library of Congress Cataloging-in-Publication is available
ISBN 978-1-61902-275-1

Cover design by Ann Weinstock

COUNTERPOINT
1919 Fifth Street
Berkeley, CA 94710
www.counterpointpress.com

Printed in the United States of America
Distributed by Publishers Group West

10 9 8 7 6 5 4 3 2 1

To Berta and George Gutekunst

Lovely thou art, to hold me close and kisst,
Now cry the birds out in the meadow mist,
Despite the cuckold, do thou as thou list,
So swiftly goes the night,
    And day comes on!

—Ezra Pound

DOUBLE HONEYMOON

MUHLBACH, having locked his front door and tested it, stands for a moment on the horsehair welcome mat to consider the neighborhood. It is Christmas Night, overcast, somewhat warmer than the newspaper has predicted—as if winter's annual victory might not yet be complete. Holiday celebrations persist, but they are subdued now. Music can be heard, evergreens glitter conspicuously in windows facing the street, and no doubt the drinking goes on; nevertheless Christmas is all but finished. Tomorrow the offices reopen. Tomorrow the clerks take charge. Tomorrow I must pledge allegiance to monotony.

Well! he remarks aloud, loud enough that the next-door cat looks at him quickly. Well, he goes on to himself, if the demise of Christmas seems a bit depressing, at least the children have been satisfied. Peppermint canes, bayberry candles, gummed stickers of Santa and lots of gold foil stars on the packages, sugarplum fairies, reindeer dancing down a blue north wind—this is what Christmas means to them. Nor could we persuade them it has a different meaning, even if we wished to. Soon enough, by themselves, they'll find out. I wonder if it could be for the children that we commemorate this day. Or for ourselves? Hmm. Once a year maybe, stuffed with good works, we attempt to resurrect the joy of crunching a candy cane harder than the unfortunate turkey's leg. Yes, that could be.

And having settled his gloves against his fingers he walks deliberately, with a thoughtful expression, between the blackened drifts of snow. There is no one else in sight.

At the corner he pauses, extends an arm beneath the streetlight to look at his watch. Six-fifteen. Within five minutes the bus should appear, another ten minutes and he will be deposited at 83rd Street. Therefore he will reach his destination precisely on time. Naturally they will be looking for him just at that time because they know him. They know he is never early, never late.

Six-fifteen and a spatter of seconds. Wouldn't it be nice, Muhlbach reflects, if the bus were late. Then I'd have something to say, an excuse to make. As it is I've no excuses, no apologies, no remarkable adventures to recount. My life has been so quiet. I suppose I should be thankful. Yes, by and large I'd have to say I'm lucky. Good health. Few debts. Nothing threatens me, unless it's the knowledge of how time passes. Very little happens, or seems to, yet the days have been evaporating. I grow older and nobody asks how I am, it's assumed I must be fine. Nobody asks how business is going, not more than once do they ask. Who cares about the details of yesterday's transaction? Would you, for instance, be particularly interested in the clauses of a policy worked out between Metropolitan Mutual and Algonquin Savings and Loan? Ah! Yes, naturally, you've got to run. Of course, of course, I understand. We'll discuss it some other time.

Across the street a door opens briefly but nobody steps outside. Then the door closes, shutting off the music and the light and the laughter.

The bus is not in sight. He begins to wonder if the noise of its engine will reach him before it turns the corner. Or does the bus have a flat tire? Is it stuck in a snowdrift? Could it have collided, by some mischance, with a subway train? Been attacked by a band of ravenous wolves from Long Island? In any case, he thinks, the bus will be at least a little late and therefore, thank God, so shall I.

Six-seventeen, almost.

Who'll be there? A small gathering, Dolly has insisted, nothing presumptuous. But that could mean—let's see, last year she assured me of this with some similar phrase and there were a hundred guests. Still, a crowd means anonymity; I could leave early, if I chose. Who'd miss me? However, she did say this would be for supper, meaning there won't be more than ten or twelve. Eula will be there, she's a close friend of Theodore. And she's after me, no mistake, though I should think that by now she'd have given up. Is it specifically me that Eula wants, or am I just a suitable candidate? Perhaps I should ask. Either way I've had marriage enough for a while. That's not the truth. Ours was richly arranged, a medieval tapestry, ornate patterns of each coming and going, bugles from afar. The prince arrives, the queen departs. Stags, hounds, birds, cats, and Greasy Joan to keel the pot. That was a plentiful life, more than this, I've not had half enough. Be honest. But how would I fare with Dame Eula? Unquestionably it's marriage that she wants, passionately desires, and if I'm to be the necessary adjunct without which she cannot achieve that blessed state—say I should be that but nothing more, couldn't I benefit even so?

Ah, here it comes! No, not the bus. A truck. A truck driving along this desolate snowbound street. How strange. At this hour, in this place, altogether strange. Muhlbach watches the truck turn a corner and vanish, looks down at the tread imprinted on the recent snow and finds that somehow he is affected by the strength those tires have registered. Few machines are more convincing than a truck. And he feels envious of the driver who knows not merely where he is going, but why.

Now as to Dolly's supper, who'll be there? Eula Cunningham by reason of the mysterious, or not so mysterious, conspiracy of womankind. Yes, Eula will be present, very much present, solid as a sausage wrapped in satin, ripe as last Sunday's gardenia. The Forsyths, probably. If so, all right, and if not—just then a dark fleet shape, a bird, perhaps, twists violently overhead and is gone. He wonders if it might have been some midwinter hallucination. No sensible creature would leave its nest tonight.

Once again he looks at his watch. Then he waits, gazing toward the end of the lifeless frozen street. The overcast is immense and oppressive; the earth turns evenly on its course.

From an open window a potpourri of voices float down the river wind, obliging him to listen although he does not want to; and such a feeling of isolation rises up in him that he grinds his heel on the pavement. Reaching out with one gloved hand he slaps the metal streetlight as militantly as though he wore a gauntlet. But how useless! What a foolish act. Startled by what he has done, he wonders that any man such as himself, long accustomed to self-control, can be so easily turned to abstract gestures. Suppose at that moment he were being watched, what must the watcher think? Here we have a man handsomely muffled in an expensive overcoat, scarfed and hatted sans reproach, standing at the bus stop—a man who, for no evident reason, reaches forth to smack the streetlight. There's no doubt that such a man is mad, no doubt at all.

Very well, Muhlbach reflects, I'm mad. I am damned and I am mad. What next? One supper party follows another. Why do I accept?

He thinks of the previous night, remembering the squandered hours. Worse than merely squandered, how altogether disagreeable that evening was! Insults enough for twenty. It might have been a plot, except that plots imply some basic logic. No, it's just the nature of that couple; they might be prototypes of the coming era, God help us. Karen's interminable account of her visit to the gynecologist—gross at any time, why did she tell about it during the meal? Maybe all of us are mad, he thinks. Either that or I'm out of joint. Do I belong to some earlier age? I might have lived more at ease in the tranquil humors of an Edwardian salon when men got to their feet half-religiously each time a lady entered. Yes, I suspect that's the case. The world's not at fault, mea culpa. I value dead fashions. Now it's not poor taste to discuss vaginal explorations, sexual encounters, or anything else. In fact it's considered 'smart.' What a paradox.

Six-twenty-one. The bus *is* late. Muhlbach stamps his feet to find out if they are frozen because it's not quite so warm as he thought when he stepped out the door. Stamping his feet causes them to sting a little, which is reassuring, and his thoughts spiral back to last night's supper—to the abominable tablecloth which had not been pressed after it was washed, and it hadn't been washed for many meals. Could this be the newest sophistication? Stains, ashes, used napkins, what's the sense of it? Was Karen oblivious? Indifferent? Was she demeaning herself? Her husband? The guest?

Muhlbach glances up, his meditations interrupted by the arrival of the bus.

Once aboard he arranges himself by a window, stretches out his legs to the heating vent, and looks about. There are no other passengers. Well well, this is luxury indeed, a private bus. The driver didn't open his mouth, not even to say Merry Christmas, but still there was no feeling of animosity. Very good, let's ride along in silence. A splendid way to travel.

He looks out the window. Snowy trees, colored light bulbs, trash cans, apartment buildings grimly cemented together. The bus is peaceful and quiet and warm, and he begins to wish that he might go riding around the city all night; he feels a sudden admiration, very close to affection, for the horsepower and comfort and majesty of this machine which voyages imperturbably through the snowy waste. Who could have devised such an excellent bus!

Another intersection, a red signal dangling above the arctic. Not a car in view, nevertheless we must wait. How extraordinarily red, how terribly violent and red is the red light. No doubt it's true that habit dulls the edge of perception; many familiar things we neglect to notice. How often have I waited for exactly such a light as this? Yet only now, as though until this moment I had been blind, do I see its color. And then qute magically it turns green! Never, he thinks while staring at the light, never never never have I seen a circle of glass so marvelously green.

The bus rolls forward, pulls itself around the corner to 79th; and Muhlbach, at ease on his plastic throne, amuses himself by breathing against the window. The ephemeral silver cloud reminds him of Karen's dress. He begins to wonder how she contrived to get inside of it. There's a chance that Dominic wrapped it around her like a flag around a skeleton, unrolling her when it was time for bed. Her outer elegance was grotesque, if not worse, compared to the filthy tablecloth. And beneath the table their ancient white poodle in its rhinestone collar, coughing up food and industriously sniffing everyone's legs. Or the half-eaten licorice dumped in his lap by Karen's sticky child, the get of previous marriage. And each insult was regarded as 'amusing.' Dominic and Karen, formidably sophisticated, referring to Christmas as The People's Midwinter Festival, exchanging presents a day early so that on Christmas Eve their guests can't help but feel somewhat bourgeois. Well, let's hope Dolly's party will be less demanding.

Six-twenty-eight. He feels the bus begin to skid. The ponderous machine arches toward the curb. All at once, as though the earth had trembled, it stops. The driver's cap sails graciously off his head and a cascade of snow probably shaken from a tree comes thundering down on the roof. The driver hops out of his seat in order to retrieve his cap. That's the important thing—the cap. Then, looking around, he inquires if his passenger is all right.

Muhlbach nods.

The driver mutters something derogatory about the street cleaning crews, whose fault this is.

Away they go, shooting a yellow light. The driver wishes to prove that the accident has not spoiled his nerve.

Well, there's a suitable topic for conversation. No doubt everybody at the party will be anxious to supply a story about bus drivers. Though if tonight's affair is as confused and frenetic as Dolly's previous parties it won't be necessary to say a word.

Before long the bus stops again, but not for a traffic light. This time we have a new passenger, presumably female, bundled to the ears in a raccoon coat from the bottom of which protrudes a pair of oleaginous white rubber boots. Muhlbach, curious, watches the figure approach. It is indeed a female, quite young, with mascaraed eyes and very pale pink lipstick. She seats herself across the aisle and he continues to look at her. He cannot imagine why she is alone; some quality about her implies a need for male companionship. That is to say, a college boy. A fraternity boy. Preferably an athletic hero. This year's quarterback. Your run-of-the-mill Rhodes Scholar, for instance, wouldn't earn a second glance. But what is she? Not a student. Possibly a chorus girl starting off to work. She appears to be no more than nineteen, though it's hard to guess because so little of her is visible and most of that has been touched up with paint. He studies her profile. Although quite delicate it has an unpleasant aspect. One might even say 'antagonistic.' Everything considered, not a particularly appealing girl.

Then she turns to look at him with hatred gleaming clearly in her eye. She gets up, not having spoken a word, and walks down the aisle to be near the driver.

Muhlbach resumes looking out the window but he does not see much; he knows that if he had said anything—even 'Merry Christmas!'—he would have been in danger. The humiliation is poisonous, it clings to him like a roach. What have I done? he asks himself. Of what am I guilty? Good God, I've been accused, judged, and condemned! He stares at his hands, mildly folded in his lap. I violated nothing, he thinks. I didn't insult that girl, I would never knowingly insult anyone. But I've been threatened. She warned me. A single word to the keeper of the bus, then what? What on earth is happening here? Am I at the mercy of every strange woman?

Angrily, suffocated by the belief that he has been treated unjustly, he glares along the aisle but cannot distinguish any more than he did at first. The enormous raccoon coat—so quaintly out of date that its hour has come around again. That and the shining hair. Her head is turned aside in order to conceal everything from the possible sex maniac. Not even the contour of her cheek remains. And the silence is a charged, living oath: her thought is bent against him.

He begins to study the reflection of himself in the

window. This translucent face which comes and goes, dependent on passing lights, what would a stranger make of it? No beard, no suggestion of eccentricity, nor even of any very great individuality. Here sits a man some forty or forty-five years of age who might be a research chemist or a physician, appropriately dressed for a winter night, spectacles firmly fixed on a bony ascetic nose—the nose of a librarian or of a Jesuit. In other words, there's nothing much to see. Nothing startling. Nothing that could honestly be called indicative of the inner man. Certainly nothing to suggest that this personage might be obsessed with violence. On the contrary, one would guess that such a reserved and placid citizen probably spent his days at Metro Mutual.

So that's all she could have deduced from appearances. Or did I speak to her? he wonders. Have I been so preoccupied that, not knowing what I did, I spoke? It's possible. Without meaning to, I might have spoken. No, it isn't possible. I'd have heard myself. In fact I've done that before, just as I've heard myself start to snore as I fell asleep. So I didn't speak, she loathes me because I looked at her. Incredible! Fortunately we won't have to put up with each other much longer. In the meantime, though, I think I'd better make a point of ignoring that disagreeable child. She might sense me staring and I can't say I'd enjoy a second confrontation.

He reaches inside his overcoat, feeling the way clumsily because of his gloves, and at last extricates the travel brochure that he has been carrying around for several weeks. He unfolds it and begins to study the map of North America, no bigger than a postcard. The map is colored like a rainbow. Honduras is lemon yellow, Mexico the color of a tangerine. Guatemala stands out—as intensely red as coral. Guatemala appears to be by far the handsomest and most appealing of these Central American nations; all routes converge on Guatemala. Muhlbach turn his attention to the local map. Antigua. Lake Atitlán. Tajumulco. Puerto Barrios. There's no doubt that Guatemala is the place to go, the place to enjoy life. And so easy to reach. Only three hours by air from New Orleans, four hours from Houston or Los Angeles.

Contemplating this waxy advertisement, he wonders why he picked it up. Because it was available? Because while walking through the lobby of the Bergmann after a particularly stultifying business lunch he saw it, brighter than a new flag at the ends of the earth?

Well, the climate of Guatemala is marvelous. Ask anybody who has been there. The highlands with an altitude of five thousand feet enjoy a year-round temperature in the seventies. The traveler will be comfortable with a lightweight coat or a sweater in the evening. The exchange of money is simple since the monetary units of Guatemala correspond to those of the United States, the quetzal being on a parity with the dollar. Nor is language a problem. Although Spanish is the national language, English is widely spoken and every employee of the Bergmann El Mirador is bilingual. Tourist cards may be obtained through any airline serving the area. This and a smallpox vaccination certificate are the only documents you will need. Should you be traveling on business, a passport and visa will be required.

Muhlbach studies a photograph of a typical room at the El Mirador in Guatemala City. It is decorated in red and saffron with draperies from ceiling to floor, furniture quite modern, a vase of flowers, a telephone, a balcony giving out to the famous mountains.

Here is a world of comfort and quiet where tasteful decor blends with contemporary convenience and luxury, with sprightly Central American color and native materials. The dining room offers superb cuisine—from exciting flaming specialties to delicious native dishes—all expertly prepared by master chefs from carefully selected foods. In the evening, romantic Latin music and entertainment set the mood for a wonderful night of relaxing, listening, and dining. A wonderful experience in hotel living awaits you in this picturesque country of timeless heritage. Luxuriously furnished guest rooms, de luxe and quiet, away from the bustle of the city. The cosmopolitan bar serves your favorite beverages prepared with the finest liquors. You'll want to prolong your stay in this welcome retreat from daily cares.

He examines other pictures. The private banquet hall, bleak and rectilinear, as though once upon a time it may have been used for storage. The cocktail lounge, with swollen leather stools and a framed painting of a matador on bended knee, flourishing his cape while narrowly eluding the charge of a prodigious black bull. The bartender, who wears a jacket with huge lapels, gazes somewhat morosely toward the camera; he would much rather be somewhere else. And the swimming pool. Beside the swimming pool a waitress in colorful native costume has delivered drinks to a handsome young Nordic couple, both of whom are beaming. There are striped umbrellas in the background. Finally we have a panorama of the main dining room; however there aren't quite enough diners—which gives it the desolate air of all dining rooms in all resort hotels off season.

The bus slows down, skidding a little. Muhlbach, very sensitive now to this motion, glances toward the driver as the surest indication of whether they are headed for another accident. But the driver does not appear tense, just watchful.

Presently he discovers that because of the travel brochure he has ridden several blocks too far. He pulls the cord immediately and gets off at the next stop. It will be a few minutes' walk back to 83rd but quicker than waiting for another bus. He notes the time, six-forty, feels mildly pleased that he will arrive a trifle late, and begins his walk. The weather has changed. It's colder, noticeably colder.

Yes, I could arrange to go, he tells himself, and slaps his gloves together. I could exchange the dollar for the quetzal—not any great amount of dollars, but enough—and I could take a room at El Mirador. Why shouldn't I? Actually, why not?

At the corner he waits for some cars to pass, then crosses against the light. Flakes of snow twirl in front of him, as pristine and friendly as those that fell on Walden Pond. A siren in the distance—but the waves are long, descending, diminishing.

Why not? Why shouldn't I? he repeats. And he continues to argue with himself about the feasibility of a little vacation in Guatemala.

By the time he has reached 84th he is aware that he is being followed. Or at least somebody has been walking the same direction at the same speed, which is probably the case. So he does not turn around but proceeds along the row of brownstones, peering at the numbers. It has been a year since he was in this neighborhood, and brownstone apartments are very nearly indistinguishable.

Having found the number he climbs the steps cautiously. The steps have been salted; even so, there's no sense being reckless.

At the top of the steps, at the entrance, he hesitates. Then he turns around and is surprised, and yet not really surprised, to see the raccoon coat. Even from this distance, from half a block, he can tell that she is watching him. She stops at once, pretending to hunt for something in her purse.

Muhlbach angrily presses the button and stamps his feet while waiting for the door to open. As soon as it does he steps inside. Then for a moment he permits himself to be suffused by rage. Why was she following him? Why? What does she want?

Then the sumptuously carpeted hall distracts him, and the odor of damp woollens—as though another guest had just recently passed through. He peels off his gloves, folds them, and tucks them into his pocket. He removes his coat, his scarf, and his hat, strides across the hall and rings for the elevator.

He frowns at himself in the monstrous gilded mirror without knowing quite why he should feel so displeased; after all, the girl was merely a nuisance. At that instant the front door springs open and she walks in. There is only bitterness on her face. It's plain that she knows, having realized it sooner than he, that they have been invited to the same party. Yet even this knowledge has failed to soften her; she looks, if possible, even more suspicious and churlish.

Muhlbach rings again for the elevator while she waits beside the door, ready to flee. It must be my age, he decides. That's why she mistrusts me. If I were ten years younger she'd have smiled.

Down comes the elevator at last and halts with a mechanical thump. The cage slides greasily open. He waits for her to enter. Without a word, with no change of expression, surrounded by that implacable cloud of hostility, she steps in; after which he steps in and the cage comes trundling shut to enclose them. We are, he reflects, like a couple of ill-tempered animals, a lion and a tigress perhaps, on our way to the circus.

Laboriously the elevator does what it was meant to do, rising eventually to the proper floor. The cage slides open, they are released.

Along the corridor side by side, with nothing whatsoever to discuss, to all appearances a man and wife. Or a girl walking beside her uncle.

At Dolly's apartment Muhlbach touches the square gold button and once again they must wait, transfixed by still another closed door. What if it does not open? What then?

Moments go by like centuries. What's the magic phrase? This must be the place. Surely this must be the place. God save me, he thinks, if I'm mistaken. And he is careful not to look at her because there's no way of knowing how she might react. But regardless of whose apartment this is, whether it belongs to Dolly or somebody else, the girl certainly intended to come here. So the question arises as to why she rode past her stop. My own reason was simple—I wasn't paying attention. But it's unlikely that she forgot, she's too conscious of everything around her. She deliberately rode beyond 83rd. She rode beyond 83rd for some specific purpose and I can think of nothing except that she didn't want to get off first, afraid that I might follow her. How much farther would she have gone in order to lose sight of me? Yet here we are, having kept our appointment in Samarra. Well, so be it.

The door is opened by a maid dressed in black. Not far behind the maid is the hostess, Dolly, encrusted with pearls and diamonds, glittering in triumph. Yes indeed, this is the place.

Dolly, stretching forth both shriveled crooked hands, calls out harshly like a very old bird, not a finch or a mockingbird or a cuckoo, but perhaps an ancient white heron:

Lambeth dear! Karl! How nice you've met! Do come in!

Well, there's no point in contradicting her. Besides, she's right, says Muhlbach to himself. Indeed we have met. So let us enter as a couple, gravely estranged. I imagine we'll head for different corners.

First there are introductions, whoever is unfortunate enough to be in the vicinity.

Dee Borowski and Sandy Kirk. Lambeth Brent. Karl Muhlbach. Or do you know each other? I'm so absent tonight. Lambeth sweet, please help yourself to the food, we're doing it buffet this year. And if you see my Theo—now where could he have gone? Oh! Charles! How delightful! Mildred dear! You look divine. I want you to meet Karl Muhlbach.

How do you do. It's a pleasure.

And Eula Cunningham? Oh! Goodness, how silly of me! And this is Jack Baxter.

Yes, we're acquainted.

I say! Hello!

Yes. The British auto salesman, Muhlbach thinks while shaking hands. The professional Englishman right down to the toothy smile and walrus mustache. I wonder how many Austins he's sold since we met, wherever it was, at some party like this, I suppose.

Baxter drifts away just as Eula reappears with an offering—a gigantic shrimp skewered on a toothpick.

Ah ha! Eula, once again you've saved my life. Now would you tell me something. That impressive personage across the room, who's he?

Do you mean Buford Atwater?

I've no idea what the man's name is. The one in the scarlet vest. With the silky Van Dyke a bit discolored by nicotine and the gold chain slung across his paunch, with a voice like a Napoleonic cannon, leaning on the carved ivory cane. Will that do? Who's he? What's the story on him?

Eula replies confidentially: I thought you knew. I thought everyone knew.

Not I, says Muhlbach somewhat more crisply than he had intended. I must admit I've never laid eyes on anything quite like that.

Few of us have, Eula murmurs. But still, I thought surely you'd recognize him. He's the raison d'être, so to speak.

Come come, Eula. Is he Beelzebub? You've lost me. What's the fellow's name?

A. Telemann Veach, she whispers, implying that one

should be knowledgeable enough to recognize the lion.

So Dolly has bagged another celebrity. Has she a chart upstairs on which the conquests are listed?

Himself! Eula adds, just in case there should be any doubt.

Are there a great many imposters? But Eula, gazing at A. Telemann Veach as if he were a statue, evidently doesn't hear. All right, let it go. What's his game? He doesn't look like the neighborhood TV repairman. Is he a high diver? Does he escort maiden schoolteachers through Africa? It would be hard to imagine Mr. Veach doing much of anything from nine to five. Be good enough to tell me, Eula, don't keep me dangling.

She seems reluctant to come straight out with the information, probably because she intends to squeeze a little more juice from this moment.

Perhaps he's wealthy? Could Mr. Veach be the descendant of somebody who invented something?—the hairpin, let's say, or the paper clip. Which is why he's entitled to wear a colorful vest.

Mr. Veach is *quite* the literary figure.

Oh? Muhlbach replies, glancing again at the great panjandrum who, just then, happens to be looking at him. Well, is Mr. Veach a critic? Does he edit some august journal? Is he a professor of Literature?

Eula pretends disbelief. Goodness, I thought you'd have him placed by now! Mr. Veach is the author of dozens of books—many of which have been translated into foreign languages. Everybody knows who he is.

This last point may be disputable, but never mind. Tell me, Eula, that initial 'A'—what does it stand for?

Abercrombie.

Impossible! Up from the past swarm those fearful names, writhing like alligators, names to haunt a boy throughout his life regardless of whether he lives in obscurity or in the winking light of fame. Names that can never never be forgotten. Abercrombie! And all at once Muhlbach discovers that he can feel no animosity toward Mr. Veach in spite of his vulgar vest. There's a man in anguish. Shades of Fauntleroy. Curses on every parent.

I believe I might like to meet him.

He's awfully rude.

So you've talked to him, have you?

We were introduced not long before you arrived. By the way, who is that girl?

Which girl?

Stop stalling. Lambeth.

Oh! Lambeth.

I insist on knowing everything about her.

Then you'll have to ask somebody else, I'm much more interested in Veach. Why do you say he's rude?

All celebrities are rude. There's something gauche about drawing attention to one's self at the expense of others. How long have you known her?

Lambeth? Oh, many years.

Not many. She's just a child. Ordinarily I believe whatever you say because you have almost no sense of humor, but now I suspect you of lying. I want you to confess. How did you meet her? Confess.

And Eula goes right along without waiting for an answer while Muhlbach sips a drink, munches another shrimp which the maid has brought around on a silver tray, and contemplates the party. It occurs to him that already he has subordinated himself to the temper of the crowd. As a matter of fact, without pausing to think about it, he agreed to exchange himself for a more gregarious imitation of himself the instant he walked through the door. His natural expression has been replaced, or at least altered sufficiently to suggest that he would rather be here than anywhere else—which is not so. Even the rhythm of his speech has been affected, and his choice of words. He reflects that for now, and until he leaves, he has committed himself to easy responses, to the exercise of useful platitudes.

Gazing about, half listening to Eula's monologue and nodding at appropriate moments, he observes a distinct break in the party. As though there were two magnetic poles, each attracting molecules. A flash of scarlet proves that Abercrombie is the center of one crowd, but who or what is the force behind the other? Some new delicacy? The anchovy dip? A fresh tray of shrimp? No, it's a person—a diminutive Latin male, impeccably tailored, wearing a black pinstripe suit, with eyes brighter than a squirrel's and a nose like Pinocchio. He smiles brilliantly, this one, he very much likes such adulation. He would be delighted to stay all night, surrounded by admirers. Now who would he be? A Captain of Industry from the banana latitudes? Eula should know. And she does, of course.

That is Señor Rafael López y Fuentes.

Now really, this is too much! This is altogether preposterous. In one corner we have the celebrated Abercrombie Veach. His opponent for this evening's match: Señor Rafael López something. What was that name again?

López y Fuentes.

All right, who is he?

The ambassador from Honduras.

Not so, according to a nearby voice. Señor López y Fuentes is the former Honduran vice-consul, now acting as special representative of the president.

In any case he seems to be running second to the burly author. And does either of them recognize what they are doing to the party? Although, of course, the fault is not exactly theirs. They are what they are, each illuminating a certain sphere simply because they cannot do otherwise, and if the neutrons surrounding them flow this way or that—well, who's to blame? But suppose they do know? Suppose they recognize the impact of their personalities, how it affects the homogeneity of the gathering? Do they care? Neither acknowledges the other. Because of pride? Apprehension? Does the runner risk a glance across his shoulder? Or to each of them is it a matter of indifference? Each in his own fashion is accustomed to being surrounded like a rare leopard in a zoo, the one by virtue of his odd accomplishment, the other because he represents Power. This latter specimen, Muhlbach judges, is equal in magnitude to the president of Yale, let's say, or the chairman of the board of a moderately large coal company. And God's lonely man, the renowned scribe, progenitor of numerous novels translated into various foreign languages, what is his equivalent? An Olympic middleweight boxing champion? A paroled gangster? A metropolitan disc jockey? The first Sherpa to scale Everest?

Eula, what's your opinion of Abercrombie's books? Ah, I see. Very little time for reading. Yes, to be sure.

Well then, what are some of the titles? Oh. Yes, of course, I'll do that. Yes, no doubt the librarian could give me a complete list.

From across the room Lambeth has been watching. Before she turns away they look into each other's eyes, and Muhlbach perceives that she is not quite so hostile. It must be that she has made a few inquiries, has been told that he is not Bluebeard. So she has been thinking over the situation, evaluating him. Muhlbach cannot restrain a moment of fantasy. What might happen if they should meet again? But they will not. Anyway, the relationship would be inhibited by more than age; indeed, that never was the cause. One fine day she might go to live with a man much older than herself, each to indulge their heart's desire. Charge accounts, furs, jewels and expensive surprises for her; the limpid sexuality of youth for him. No, it's not just a problem of age. When I was twenty, he reflects, I met this girl but she found me unbearably dull—dull and a trifle cold, my spine too rigid when we went dancing, my interests too academic. I'd talk of astronomy or of Hegel. No wonder I lost. And I'd lose again.

Around him the party runs its course. Occasionally someone approaches to chat and he responds, putting on his best face. Eula is seldom far away and he feels grateful to her, not just because she returns from each excursion with another morsel of food but because she usually seems to be present when the recipe calls for a spoonful of utterly meaningless conversation. She can always ladle out something to fill a silence. She's good at that, he thinks. I wish I could do it. But I'm like a foreigner speaking a different language. I'm thoroughly out of place at these affairs. Who can I talk to?

As though summoned by the question, Abercrombie Telemann Veach heaves into view, reeking of cigar smoke and gin, rumbling and belching, one blistering blue eye trained on Muhlbach and the other eye wandering.

You're in the market, says Veach. I can spot 'em right away.

Does he mean the stock market? No. No, you've got me confused with somebody else.

Okay, you're not in the market. What's your trade?

I'm considered an expert on corporate fire insurance. Metropolitan Mutual. Here, let me give you my card. And feeling rather absurd, moved by a force he does not understand, he offers the card.

Without so much as a glance at it Veach tucks the card into his vest pocket; obviously it will soon find a home in an ashtray. Eula was right, the man is rude.

I figured you for a broker.

No, I'm not. But I happen to have a few investments, so I do pay a certain amount of attention to the financial scene.

Ever hear of a stock called Taggo?

I can't say that I have.

Veach scowls. Some son of a bitch has been touting me. You make a few bucks and they start to crawl out of the woodwork. Jesus Christ! he mutters and grinds the tip of his cane into the rug. If it ain't one thing it's sure as hell another. Last week it was some Goddamned abandoned silver mine in Arizona fifty miles from Prescott. The metal's there, this nance tells me, only there's a few feet of water in the shaft. They need five grand to pump out the water. Five grand! I told him to go lap it up.

What information have you on this Taggo stock?

They make a labeling gadget. Sell the bloody thing in the dime store. Sell millions, I guess. Okay, what the hell, but they don't pay any dividend. I got three wives to support, what am I gonna do with a stock that won't pay me a dividend? It'll go up, this tout swears on a Bible. Never heard of it, eh? I'm not surprised. What did you say your name was?

Muhlbach.

Is that a fact! There used to be a Muhlbach's grocery store in my neighborhood when I was a kid. You know, I don't belong in this crowd. I've gone around the world twice but still I don't belong. Veach glowers at a woman who had been about to approach; she takes a step backward and stares at him uneasily. Veach tugs his beard. Aw, he says, I'm from just a real small town. Every once in a while I think maybe I ought to try it again, but hell, I wouldn't make out any better, maybe worse. It's been so long. He shrugs, displaying his broad fat back to another admirer. Goddamned sycophants, he mumbles. You wouldn't believe what I put up with. The only decent thing that happened all year was the Horizon Book Club. He inspects Muhlbach to see if this brings a reaction. Don't know my stuff, do you? Christ, I can tell. You're a morning paper man. Financial section. Editorial. No comics. That's about the size of you. Sure. In fact I bet you read murder mysteries.

Occasionally, yes. As a soporific.

Aw, crap! Soporific my ass! Come off it, Muhlbach. You love that garbage. I know all about you. You haven't opened a real novel in the past five years.

I don't read many novels. Contemporary novels especially.

What's the matter with contemporaries?

Well, how does one explain? Say that today's authors seem tortured, frenetic, shallow? Empty of *fond?* Say that they do not know how to write of the world and its magic but merely of themselves? Say that they are, in a word, tiresome?

This interests Veach. I'll be a son of a bitch, says he.

Muhlbach, stimulated by the response, decides to continue. When he does read it is apt to be the essays of Hazlitt, or perhaps a novel as richly variegated and weathered as an autumn leaf. In these books one discovers dignity and grace, qualities now scorned. One finds eloquence, intellect, chastity of mind, courtesy, and a conviction that tomorrow morning as usual the sun will rise. Yes, these things exist; old authors knew them. Now they have been abandoned and derided. Now it's stylish to shock the reader, yet therein lies a fallacy, because in these times all sensitive readers have been benumbed, no further shocks are conceivable. In any case, Muhlbach adds, he seldom reads. Listening to music seems more rewarding. Haydn. Monteverdi. Grillparzer. Palestrina. Purcell. Scarlatti. So many excellent composers, each in his way as remunerative as his predecessor.

Hell, that's all right, says Veach. Music's okay. Those guys and I work the same racket, only we use different tools.

Would he be familiar with Telemann? Probably. Yes, of course. Even though he himself may not care for classical music he must have acquaintances who do, who would have presented him with the Passions, the suites for woodwinds, strings, and horns, the sonatas of his namesake.

Maybe you're better off not reading, says Veach. I mean that. There's so much crap in print. I ought to know, I'm responsible for plenty of it. Take these dumb broads, he goes on without lowering his voice and gestures at the nearest woman. They buy any sort of bilge. The worse it is the better they like it. Now me, for instance, I've had three novels on the *Times* best seller list—half a million hardbacks on the first one. Half a million! Cranked out for no reason except money. I'm good at that. I earn so much I'm amazed. Gross, for God's sake, not net. After the government's finished throwing out my deductions I might as well be a drugstore clerk. I've hired a dozen shysters but the Feds still crucify me. Also, try chopping up royalties among three wives and count what's left. Hell, it wouldn't feed a terrier for a week. I guess I do better than most, though. Maybe. I don't know. Some days I just don't know. Veach exhales, grunts, and scratches himself. He upends his cane and seems to be examining the tip. By any chance, Muhlbach, have you got a cigar?

No.

I could send one of these biddies out to fetch me a cigar and she'd love it. Tell her biddy friends what an awful person I am. Christ, I know them like I know the back of my hand. Run around quacking. Quack quack quack. Aw, well. Listen, Muhlbach, it's a mighty peculiar profession when a man can work his balls off for a book he believes in and then be ignored. For instance, you take these harlequins that call themselves critics. You know what they are? I'll tell you. What they are is Eastbay minnow fishermen. They wouldn't know an original work of art if it jumped up and grabbed them by the nipple. You know how they refer to me? The 'aging challenger.' I spent four years on a novel, revised the son of a bitch till my eyes felt like bubble gum. Did the critics realize what was in that book? Let me tell you. Confused! That's what they decided. Can you imagine? Mr. Veach's heroic attempt is, to put it kindly, confused. How the hell would they know? Three-fourths of them would get confused by McGuffey.

So this is what he wants, Muhlbach reflects. The approval of literary critics. I should think money and publicity would be enough. He has both, more than other people dream about, much less anticipate. And still he feels neglected, shortchanged. Incredible!

Aw, you don't care. But why should you? I mean nothing to you, you mean nothing to me. Nobody cares what happens to anybody else. They say they do but they don't. I been around the track too many times, I can't be fooled. Veach stabs the rug here and there with his ivory cane, half-mortal blows. Then, after a meditative belch, he announces that he might as well see what there is to eat, and he limps away—pushing through the crowd toward the silver platters.

Eula reappears. She must have been somewhere nearby waiting for the uncouth author to leave. Probably she attempted to be sociable and was rewarded with a shattering insult. In any case she doesn't mention him; Lambeth is on her mind. She has been gone no more than ten minutes but she has accumulated enough information to begin a dossier.

Lambeth wears a size ten dress and has been seen more than once shopping at Gimbel's. She attended City College, studied dramatics, did not do especially well and left after three semesters. She is twenty years old. She lived for a number of months in Greenwich Village, where it is said she had some sort of unnatural affair. This past summer she became engaged to a young Navy man stationed at Pensacola who, not long ago, was tragically killed in an airplane crash. She is a heavy drinker, although not many people know this. As a matter of fact she is at this moment in the kitchen well on her way to being drunk, talking to the servants. But getting back to essentials, her reputation very definitely is not of the best. There are rumors that she gave quite a performance for a group of fliers in the Westbury Hotel.

Muhlbach listens in amazement.

Eula continues. Lambeth's mother lives in Brooklyn Heights, her father died some years ago of a heart attack. He was considerably older than Lambeth's mother. He was in the garment business. He lost a small fortune during the big depression. Lambeth has a sister, eighteen, whose name is Judith. She also has a brother, whose name Eula could not find out, who is either fourteen or fifteen and is attending military school in Wisconsin.

Eula, after pausing for a sip of sherry, goes on. Lambeth's eye shadow is by Helena Rubenstein, mascara by Topique. Coiffure by Mister Francis. She adores the Gilded Grape.

Muhlbach interrupts. What is the gilded grape? Is that another way of saying she drinks a lot?

The Gilded Grape is a club. Very popular with the young set.

I see. Now what else have you discovered?

Lambeth is notoriously fickle. She is selfish. She is spoiled. She demands compliments. She can be terribly unpleasant. Her ambition is to become a high fashion model.

And what is your ambition, Eula? But the question cannot be asked, nor would any response be necessary. Eula's ambition is obvious. Marriage. Eula is ripe, and ripeness implies a slow descent toward maturation. Under the circumstances, namely that she has not yet gathered up a husband, this isn't a good thing. Statistics are not encouraging. Less than eight percent at Eula's present age will marry within the year. This isn't good. Unremitting effort is required to join that fortunate minority. Next year the percentage will be worse. So call on past experience, press the case. Fill the gentleman's wassail bowl and bring him meat.

Muhlbach, accepting another tidbit from Eula's hand, reflects that a second marriage is not impossible. Not at all. But not just now. Nor is the fair Eula a likely prospect, though of course such things must be left unsaid, to be divined. That Eula fails to divine this fact is her principal liability. Perhaps, though, she does recognize it and believes, as do all women, that she can alter the situation. How extraordinarily conceited women are.

Nine-thirty. The maid approaches with a platter of sandwiches designed for Lilliputians. In the midst of the sandwiches is a pile of hors d'oeuvres that only a cannibal could identify.

I believe I've had enough, says Muhlbach.

But it seems that the maid has another purpose. Excuse me, sir. Will you follow me, please?

He looks into the warm chocolate eye but her

thoughts cannot be discerned. Subdued by years of domestic service, she does no more than carry out her mission. One might as well expect a hint from a Kikuyu mask.

May I ask why?

Señor López y Fuentes wishes to speak to you.

Muhlbach shoots a glance through the crowd. López y Fuentes is not where he was a few minutes ago.

Are you positive?

Yes, sir. Already she has taken the first step, certain that he will follow.

López y Fuentes is alone in the hall. Quickly he smiles and holds out his hand.

What does he want? Muhlbach wonders while they exchange names and pleasantries. Does he think I'm a stockbroker? Well, whatever it is, he's anxious not to be overheard. I wish I could remember something about Honduras. Let's see, it was a nest of spies during the Second World War. They sell coffee and bananas and so forth. Beyond that—Lord, I can't remember a thing. I wonder what on earth he wants.

Señor López y Fuentes begins by coughing gently into his fist. What I have to say, he murmurs, should be regarded as confidential. I hope you will not misunderstand.

Muhlbach nods and waits. In spite of himself he feels a vague excitement. Could it be that some sort of diplomatic intrigue is under way? After all, who knows what goes on beneath the surface of parties such as this?

I am, as possibly you may be aware, a member of slight significance in the diplomatic corps.

So I've been told.

It is not often that I find myself at a loss for words.

I understand.

Thank you. It seems we have the reputation, deservedly or not, of being not merely discreet, naturally, but articulate. I therefore regret that I am a disgrace to our—what is it to be called?—'profession'? Very well, suppose we call it that.

Gazing down at the fragile punctilious Latin, waiting for him to proceed, Muhlbach feels that it is rather gross of himself to be so tall. It is almost boorish to be eight or ten inches taller than somebody else.

López y Fuentes darts a furtive look at a guest returning from the toilet.

How strange! The man seems uneasy. Whatever's on his mind, why doesn't he come right out with it? And because they cannot just stand there, Muhlbach decides to encourage the conversation:

Señor, are you familiar with Guatemala?

Guatemala! barks the diplomat. Yes. Very familiar. Of course. Then he smiles. Guatemala is our neighbor, I am happy to say. Why do you inquire?

Muhlbach, absorbed by the staccato response and the oddly squirrel-like russet eyes, cannot think of an intelligent answer. It was, after all, a senseless question. The only reason it came to mind was that he happened to have a travel brochure in his overcoat pocket.

However, the question has served its purpose. López y Fuentes is talking again:

Although it may well be true that Guatemala in the terms of geographical area is of more extensive size than my own country, we of Honduras do not consider size to be the cardinal virtue. For you here in the enormous United States, of which I have as yet been privileged to observe very little, much to my regret, each of the republics of Central America will be regarded as unusually small. But someday—and soon, I hope—you will visit to see for yourself the very many splendid examples of architecture and other attractions of which we are so proud. I have myself, unfortunately, as yet not enjoyed the beaches of California and Florida and Texas, for example, when it comes to recreation spots, but may I assure you, Mr. Muhlbach, that I believe they cannot be more enjoyable than those we possess.

The speech concludes as abruptly as it began. Señor López y Fuentes once again surveys the hall.

I have wished to speak to you, he resumes, because I am able from watching you to know that you are a man of the world, as the expression goes. Please, don't say a word. Don't protest. It is true. You will excuse me if I boast, but I have had a great deal of experience, as perhaps you imagine, in being able to estimate the character. In other words, without finding inquiries necessary I believe I am able to know what you are. Please believe this, I have asked no one about you, Mr. Muhlbach. No one. Because I consider it best to judge for myself. And I have said to myself that you are at one and the same time sophisticated, yes, a gentleman of superior intelligence. You are, above all, let me emphasize, a man who is able to respect confidence. I am positive of this. You have also—permit me to say so—the most discriminating taste. Exceptional. This is evident in the fashion of your dress, which is to say the care of your suit, but becomes, if possible, more to be praised in the selection of your companion. In other words, I have noticed you both and exclaimed to myself upon the first instant you have entered the room.

So graciously—with such a complimentary overtone—has the reference been included that for a moment Muhlbach does not recognize it for what it is. But then, mute with astonishment, he understands. Diplomatic maneuvering, yes. Intrigue, yes. Of the oldest sort. López y Fuentes has indeed undertaken a political mission. What he wants, however, is some means of access not to the Secretary of State's ear but to Lambeth.

Accept my sincere congratulations, he is saying. You are to be complimented in the highest terms, Mr. Muhlbach. Rarely if ever have I been privileged to observe a more attractive young girl. Words fail me. Yes, it's so. I compliment you upon such good fortune.

Thank you, Muhlbach replies, and wonders how he could possibly have failed to guess what was coming.

If I may be permitted, López continues. It is a young girl who can ruin us before we realize, eh? This happens, yes, I have seen it. In my country, many times. I am sure it will happen also very often in the United States. Is this not true? Furthermore, to become—no, how should I explain?—let me say that to be the victim of a beautiful young girl is not always, at least it is in my opinion, a catastrophe. Do you agree or not? Because with the sacrifice of one's self upon the altar of love there is always, of course, a certain degree of honor. So it is for one reason that the young girls of this type are in my country very popular. In other words, the Honduran is like the gentleman of sophisticated European circles. The Parisian, eh? Or the American of good taste such as yourself. We are all alike. We have the wisdom to appreciate the divine creation which has been provided to us by the device of nature. Nor do I have much fear saying these things because I know you will not take offense. If I may be permitted, I congratulate you again. This is a girl who will drive you mad.

He seizes Muhlbach by the hand.

So. The dream has popped. Here is reality. One might even call it naked reality.

Let me be honest, López murmurs with a look of brotherly affection. Frankly I must tell you that I have become very much tired—in fact I would even say 'exhausted'—by the necessity to pretend that what is of concern to me would be the state of the world. Frankly, I have reached the point where to me international affairs are of no interest. I admit this with embarrassment, yet it is true. No longer do I care! Sometimes, Mr. Muhlbach, I ask myself if even in the past I have cared. Perhaps not. There have been occasions, yes. But on the whole I would have to say no. In other words, for example, I am possibly like the young man who is able to inherit the grocery store of his father or the important factory which is manufacturing durable goods, who does not wish to spend his life doing that. I hope I make myself clear. I am, myself, although I do not mention it, of a family of nobility. It is a fact that my paternal grandfather in his life very many times has been invited to the palace and to official functions of many sorts in Tegucigalpa. He was quick to take advantage of such opportunity in order to advance himself. To do otherwise is foolish. Life is at best difficult, I'm sure you agree. Tell me about this young girl. Is she a movie starlet?

I think not.

You think not. To say that you are discreet, Mr. Muhlbach, does not do justice. Surely it is not too much to expect a more revealing answer.

We're not well acquainted.

You and I?

The girl and I.

It is regrettable that you wish to give me no information.

I have none to give.

It would be of great pleasure, I am sure, to this young lady to know how you are protecting her reputation. She also has been able to perceive, as do I, that you are without doubt a gentleman of integrity, to say the least. One in whom it is difficult to misplace confidence. Otherwise, in my opinion, she will not accept you to be her lover.

Think whatever you like.

I offend you. I am sorry. I would not have elected to approach you on this matter if I had not been able to observe from the beginning that, as the common expression goes, love takes wing. No. Excuse me. 'Love has taken wing.'

I don't understand.

Forgive me, but it has come to my attention how very seldom you have been watching what she is doing. The same is also true in the case of the lady. I therefore have said to myself that nothing ventured, nothing gained. It does not seem to me that a favor of such insignificance as the telephone number of this girl would be regarded as a serious problem.

I'm afraid you yourself will have to ask her for the number.

You will not give it to me?

Let's say that I don't know it.

Unbelievable! I have no choice, therefore, except to salute such gallantry. You understand, of course, how in my position it will be unwise to speak directly? In my position this cannot be done. Do you appreciate what I am saying?

I do.

A moment of silence. Señor López y Fuentes shrugs. There are days when nothing goes right.

She is not an actress?

I have been told that she studied dramatics.

López y Fuentes regards him carefully.

All at once, Mr. Muhlbach, I find that I think it is not your intention to deceive me. I think, in fact, you are not acquainted. I cannot explain to myself why I believe this is the case. But do you consider it possible that this girl might have accepted roles in moving pictures that are not to be viewed by the public? Would you know about this?

I would not.

Since it embarrasses you, let us drop the subject. Accept my apology. I have no desire to make the situation difficult. Perhaps you understand that because I am so tired of the life I am leading that I will give anything to escape. You have no idea. I am a desperate man because I am so bored. You could not begin to guess how I am stifled.

Stifled?

That's it, thank you. Stifled. Do you speak Spanish?

A few words.

Muy poco, eh? What a shame. We have a most beautiful language. You would enjoy reading in the original our great poets and the playwrights. Calderón de la Barca. Lope de Vega. Antonio Machado. These are names that come to mind. To say nothing of those more recent. Rubén Darío. Octavio Paz. Naturally there are too many, I could not recite all the names, but in the original you will find them exciting.

I'm sure I would.

French, however, is the language one employs to address a young lady. On certain occasions there is no substitute for French. I'm sorry you will not provide me with the least information.

Her name is Lambeth. Lambeth Brent. She has a brother who is attending military school in Minnesota or Wisconsin, I've forgotten which, who is reputed to be either fourteen or fifteen years of age. She has a sister whose name I've forgotten. The other day, or possibly last year, she purchased a size ten dress in Gimbel's department store and the name of her hairdresser is Francis. These details might interest you. Her mother, so I have been informed, through no curiosity of my own, lives in Brooklyn Heights, but I do not know that telephone number either.

Such ill temper, Mr. Muhlbach, does not become you. It is not appropriate. I confess to being surprised. However I recognize that it is the result not of your passion but of my own. Now, please, you will accept my apologies. It's plain to me that you are a sensitive man, that you have resented what you consider to be interrogation. We will drop the subject, eh?

Good.

One more word. One only. López y Fuentes steps

nearer. I wish to explain something to you so as to clear the atmosphere. Listen, my friend. What I have wished throughout my life is to become a producer of films. For this I will give anything. Yes, anything! However, fortune seems to be determining against the fulfillment of my desire, I do not know why. Do you, by coincidence, enjoy the friendship of close acquaintances in Hollywood California?

No.

You have no friends there?

Not one.

What a pity. I have heard very much about Hollywood. In fact, permit me to tell you that I am thinking of resigning my position in order to go to Hollywood. Do you think that will be a good idea? Let me express the matter in other words. Should it be possible there to form acquaintances to pave the way? In my opinion, yes, that will be possible.

López y Fuentes is no longer talking to anyone but himself. Answers aren't required. Logic has nothing to do with it: all that matters is the dream.

He holds out his hand.

Does this mean goodby? Apparently so.

A moment later the tiny diplomat has disappeared, not much daunted by his bad luck. Is he once again on the prowl for Lambeth? Or has he retreated to the security of the ordered rank, somewhat bruised but unrepentant? Five years hence will he be found in Hollywood California behind smoked glasses, or in Geneva wearing striped pants?

Well, it's time to leave. It may not be late, not long past ten, but that's late enough. Yes, Muhlbach reflects,

I'm ready. There's nothing for me here. I only wish I were on my way to Guatemala.

Searching out the hostess, he says goodnight. And goodnight to Eula. She's a trifle peevish to see him escape but there'll come another opportunity. Goodnight to Lambeth, wherever she is; goodnight in absentia, may we not meet again. Goodnight to the celebrated dyspeptic novelist who left the gala party half an hour before.

So, having sampled this evening and found it neither exhilarating nor intolerable, having retrieved his hat and scarf and coat and gloves, Muhlbach departs. Somberly, meditatively, he rides down alone in the gilded cage, opens the door to the street, and then for a moment he pauses on the windy freezing step. Overhead the clouds have parted, offering a glimpse of the December constellations, and it occurs to him again that he should get away. I should. Yes, I should, he thinks a little wildly. I really ought to go.

NEVERTHELESS it's easier to contemplate flying off to Guatemala than it is to buy a ticket. And as winter retreats, Muhlbach, turning down the thermostat, reminds himself that life in New York isn't so bad—not now, at least, when one can sense the approach of spring. Already the petty bourgeois neighborhood animals have begun to poke about, investigating this and that, prepared to resume their outdoor rounds, and cautious green shoots soon will be decorating the garden. And then for a little while before summer gets serious, during that brief pleasant season, the windows may be left wide open without attempting to calculate the liabilities and benefits—whether one should exclude the breeze along with the heat, or admit both.

But I'm going to get away, he thinks, nodding affirmatively. I might very possibly visit Central America next winter. Yes, that would be a good time. Because I do need a break, a fresh experience, a change of routine. I'm sick of this predictable existence. I'm as stiffled as that little diplomat.

Then, one evening in March while waiting for the bus, having worked late, he glances up from his folded newspaper just in time to see López y Fuentes, accompanied by a gorgeous blonde, scurry across the street. They seem to be heading for La Galette where, presumably, they will have supper. Yes. Yes, that's where they intend to go. Somewhat bemused, Muhlbach lowers the paper in order to watch.

López gallantly gives the revolving door a shove. His companion, who appears rather bored, obediently enters the welcoming quadrant and is swept away. López, after having adjusted his necktie, follows her with a look of determination. Moments later he can be observed through the plate glass window snapping his fingers with the casual arrogance of those who are accustomed to immediate service; and from the depths of La Galette an obsequious maître d'hôtel materializes like a genie, displaying a pair of tasseled menus.

After having delivered one inaudible line the maître d' marches triumphantly offstage propelled by his own importance. Next to leave is the indifferent lady. López y Fuentes, however, turns around before exiting to confront his audience with a characteristic Latin gesture—laying an index finger significantly beneath one eye. I see you!

Muhlbach, a bit startled to find himself included in the cast, is about to respond with a nod or a wave of recognition, but all at once the stage is empty. Well, he thinks, good luck López. I wouldn't mind being present for the next act, and the third one especially, but I've got other plans. Then it occurs to him that this is not true; what plans he had made aren't in the least important. However, it would be embarrassing to follow them into the restaurant. Worse than embarrassing. Impossible. Out of the question. And yet, he asks himself, why shouldn't I have supper at La Galette if I want to? He's only an acquaintance. Besides, I've heard the food is excellent. All right, I will. I'll just request a table on the opposite side of the room.

Unfortunately La Galette is full. Not a table anywhere. Reservations are the usual thing.

Good! I have no business here, he thinks. I don't know what got into me. What a silly idea.

At that moment López arrives on the scene, clearly not overjoyed, although he attempts to look delighted and to sound enthusiastic. The burden of his message is that Muhlbach must join them. The lady insists.

Seriously?

Yes. Be good enough not to argue, please.

Well, that explains his reluctant expression. He'd like nothing less than a third party at the table, particularly another man.

I appreciate the invitation, but would you mind telling me why she 'insists'?

López coughs into his fist. Excuse me. Is it possible that you have forgotten?

What have I forgotten?

The young lady.

I don't know the young lady.

Yet even as he hears himself speaking he remembers. That girl at the party. Of course. This must be the same one.

I take it back. Perhaps I do know her.

Lambeth. In case you have not recalled the name.

Yes. Brown? Bryant?

Brent.

That's it. Lambeth Brent. Well, your persistence seems to have paid off. You were anxious to congratulate me, now let me congratulate you.

Thank you. However I am obliged to admit, in confidence, as one gentleman to the other, that everything has not been what is to be expected. In other words, if I may say so, a bed of roses. There have been occasions, I do not mind telling you, of the utmost difficulty.

I can very easily believe that.

Yes. Perhaps because of the fact that she happens to be not yet in certain respects what we will call a woman. I do not know if I make myself clear.

No, you don't.

I mean to say that she is very young, as I am sure you have noticed. This may be the root of the problem. It is not unusual when one is, as we are, you and I, of a certain age. These very young girls—ah, but I am sure you understand because you are like myself a man of the world. Now come, if you please.

Muhlbach hesitates.

Quite frankly, López, I feel a trifle awkward. I wonder if there hasn't been some kind of mistake.

What do you mean, mistake?

I can't believe she wants me to join you. I've spoken to that girl only once in my life—at the party—and I got a distinct impression that she didn't care for me.

Why is this?

I have no idea.

Do you not consider her attractive?

More than 'attractive.' She's quite beautiful. Too much so for her own good.

Yet you wish to avoid her?

I have a feeling that she would prefer to avoid me. Something about me seems to irritate her, which is why I don't understand the invitation. I wonder if she might possibly have me confused with somebody else.

I think not. Because she has said to me, and these are the words: 'Rafael, go ask Mr. Muhlbach to join us.'

She did?

Permit me to reassure you that she knows beyond doubt who you are. As to why it is her wish for you to have supper with us . . .

He shrugs, spreading his graceful ivory hands.

Muhlbach frowns. I'm right about that girl, she very definitely avoided me. How strange. Although, of course, I could have misinterpreted her attitude. No. No, I didn't. This is curious. But I suppose it wouldn't hurt to take a chance. All right. Nothing ventured, as the saying goes, nothing gained.

Lead the way, López. I'd be delighted to join you.

And it is indeed Lambeth Brent. The profile, the immaculate skin, the clear crystal eye. Yet at the same time she looks different. Why didn't I recognize her? he asks himself. Does she have a new hairstyle? Yes. At Christmas it was pinned up, giving a kind of Mademoiselle de Maintenon effect. Now it's loose, parted in the center, more in keeping with her youth. But I did like that holiday arrangement—the elaborate formality of it. The elegance. The sophistication. Now she keeps pushing at it.

What else is different? For one thing, the lipstick. At Christmas her lips looked almost white, practically frosted, as though they'd been coated with vaseline. And the rest of her face—well, she must have emptied the make-up kit. Rouge, mascara, eye shadow, et cetera. The suggestion of decadence was exciting, if rather grotesque. Tonight she looks cleaner. More like a college girl than a chorine. She seems friendlier, too. None of that remote challenging hostility.

Muy bonita, eh? López asks, displaying her like a succulent fruit. Que mango!

Rafael, she complains, laying a tapered hand on his sleeve. You promised you'd stop. Mr. Muhlbach, do you know Spanish?

A word here and there. Mango, for instance.

I'm always a mango or a guapa—whatever a guapa is. I'm afraid to ask. I wish men would treat us like human beings instead of objects. I mean, women don't talk about men that way.

López, electing to play the fool, rolls his eyes.

They're really predictable, she continues, ignoring him. Like some guy will come up to me while I'm having lunch and even before he opens his mouth I know what he's getting ready to say. 'Do you eat here often?' or 'Why don't you smile?' or 'You must be in show business.' It's a drag.

What sort of comment would interest you?

He could ask what colors I like.

Muhlbach turns to López. Would that occur to you?

To ask what color is her preference? No. Frankly, I may say that in spite of many questions which will be occurring to me this will not be one. No, there will be other things on my mind. However, as to the nature of these . . .

Lambeth makes a face, yet she seems to be enjoying the discussion. Mr. Muhlbach, if you wanted to pick me up what line would you use?

I was married for such a long time that I'm afraid I'm out of practice.

You're divorced?

Widowed.

Oh wow, that's me, I always stick my foot in it. I'm sorry. I ask such dumb questions. And I was just about to ask another.

Go right ahead.

Okay then. Before you got married were you shy about picking up girls? Because you sure are the type. You probably got all tongue-tied.

López interrupts. I do not suffer from this. On the contrary, if anything, as you have observed. I do not find it difficult to speak. No, not in the least. And when there is a situation such as at present, with a beautiful woman whom we are privileged to enjoy between us at the table—in such a case, never! As a matter of fact, as you are able to guess, more often than not, I would have to say that the difficulty may be for anyone to catch my ear. Verdad?

And López continues talking, laughing, gesticulating, acting the faintly ludicrous role he has invented for himself, saying very little if anything, employing circumlocutions which are not altogether a result of his unfamiliarity with everyday English. No doubt his Spanish would be the same—convoluted sentences embellished with a variety of ribbons and streamers.

He might ramble on for an hour, Muhlbach thinks. It's as if somebody pushed a button. He's trying to hold her attention, of course, but it won't work. The girl's bored. She's picking at the tablecloth. In fact the harder he tries to entertain her the worse it's going to get. He's so observant, why can't he see that?

What do you do? Lambeth asks when her escort finally runs down. I mean, what kind of a job have you got?

Insurance. Not door-to-door exactly. I'm with Metropolitan Mutual and for the most part we handle corporation accounts. It sounds insufferably dull but I find it rather stimulating. Or at least challenging.

You really ought to go from door to door.

Muhlbach acknowledges this with a smile. Now what about yourself? I gather you're not in show business.

She answers that she is a model. But as she spoke she brushed her hair aside and glanced across the room. And there was a faint note of resistance discernible in her voice, suggesting that she hasn't been too successful, which is odd, considering those extraordinary features. How could she fail to be a success? Photographers ought to be stumbling over their equipment.

Questioned further, she becomes evasive. She would like to do high fashion, but getting started isn't easy. Last week, however, she was introduced to Rick Marquis.

And who is he?

One of the top agents. Without a top agent you might as well give up. Actually it's incredible, but everything depends on your agent. . . .

On and on she goes with the same artless evasiveness, a little too fast, a shade too cheerfully. She mentions the waiting room at the Marquis agency, flooded with girls, each one more beautiful than the last, which made her feel terribly inadequate. But then she dismisses this horde of competitors. Apparently certain stars and planets are on her side. She is a Libra and clothes look good on a Libra. Furthermore her moon is in Leo in the first House trine to Venus. As if this weren't enough, Mars is in the tenth House!

Ah ha, Muhlbach murmurs, attempting to hide his dismay.

Aren't you into astrology?

I've never paid much attention to it. Astronomy, yes.

Don't you feel there's a lot of truth in astrology?

I know nothing about it, he answers and manages to prevent himself from adding that he regards it on a par with crystal gazing and ouija boards. Astrology! The moon is in Leo, which proves things are going to get better and better every day in every way. Rick Marquis will call to say she has been picked for the cover of Cosmopolitan because Sagittarius is in opposition, or conjunction, or whatever, with the fourteenth House of David.

I'd like to introduce you to this astrologer friend of mine. I mean he's so accurate it's just uncanny . . .

And she explains about having met this prodigious forecaster while eating breakfast at Chock full o' Nuts. Muhlbach, pretending to listen, discreetly appraises her suit, which is either an exclusive Paris number or a remarkable duplicate. So she must be getting a certain amount of work. But still, exotic women always seem to be perfectly dressed. It's one of the world's trivial mysteries.

As for López, what's he up to these days?

After five minutes of circumnavigation, because he is either unwilling or unable to say anything simply, what it comes down to is that he is out of work. Waiting for the right opportunity. The job as special representative seems to have gone up in smoke. And Muhlbach feels a surge of gratitude toward whatever gods or planets have been supervising his own fortune. These past several months may not have been lucrative but at least there's hamburger on the table. López, though, just exactly how does he stay alive? A person who has been lopped from the payroll can fly only so far on credit, regardless of how polished or garrulous he may be, and López gives every indication of being an empty pocket artist.

Even more curious, why should Lambeth find such a man attractive? He must be almost twice her age, undersized, certainly not handsome. He's amiable, yes, and clever enough. A bit of a fop. Neat. Punctilious. Courteous. So there is nothing drastically wrong. Nevertheless it's puzzling; if he were rich or famous or looked like Dominguin—well, then it might be comprehensible.

Muhlbach tries to view him as a woman might, and

concludes that except for the encroaching baldness and the Pinocchio nose he could be judged reasonably good-looking. The liquid brown eyes glow with vitality. Or could that be satyriasis?—a condition which would explain quite a lot. Yes. Yes, that just might be his vial of black magic. Lambeth, however, gives an impression of distance and coolness, almost of frigidity, despite those ravishing features. And her body is slim, supple, almost lean, not the saftig body of a nymph. It would be hard to imagine her leaping into the embrace of a balding middle-aged sensualist. Indeed, López himself, contrary to what might be expected, has admitted that the affair is not altogether a bed of roses.

Well, it's an odd relationship, Muhlbach reflects while buttering a slice of bread. Furthermore I don't understand why she invited me to join them because I'm suspicious, to say the least, of that blatant invitation in her eyes. Why does she want me here? She's a beauty, though. Lord, what would it be like to have her for myself? Suppose Don Juan Rafael were dragged away, leaving just the two of us. Hah! But what would we say to each other? Of course it's been easy so far, I've enjoyed these silly table games, but how long could we handle a serious conversation? Say she were physically attracted to me, would that complicate or simplify the business? Say we were lovers. No. No, that's preposterous, I'm probably older than López. Besides, if he isn't a matinee idol he at least knows how to keep a party alive—lots of noise and little substance. That's the ticket. Whereas I have a hard time getting past today's weather. No, she and I couldn't pair off. We could be friends, perhaps. As a matter of fact I'd like that. Certainly it would be flattering, and it might be instructive because her outlook on life must be inconceivably different from my own. Also, I must admit it's delightful just to be in her presence. Each time she glances at me I feel complimented. Everybody in the place has noticed her. And she must go through life like this—being stared at day after day, night after night. How can she put up with it? I couldn't.

As soon as López stops talking Lambeth once again diverts the conversation:

Mr. Muhlbach, I guess I was pretty rude to you at Dolly's party. We probably didn't say six words to each other.

Less than six, but don't apologize.

I was really upset. I'd spent the whole afternoon with this Navy man who knew my fiancé and it turned out to be hideous. It was just all so unbelievable. I mean he—oh, I won't talk about it. But I guess I was in such a really rotten mood I took it out on you. Do you understand?

Of course.

Do you? I hope so. My fiancé was a pilot and he was killed in a crash at Pensacola.

Somebody at the party mentioned it.

I guess the whole world knows. Anyway I thought Michael was being kind and felt sorry for me so I invited him up for a drink, but then for no reason he turned into a maniac. I was terrified. I thought he was planning to strangle me. He kept calling me these awful names . . .

Suddenly, as though she had forgotten López, she asks if he would get some cigarettes. He responds with a quick venomous look. Fetching cigarettes is the waiter's job. Her face gradually congeals, indicating that it is not a request but an ultimatum. López hesitates, then jumps up, flings his napkin on the table and strides away with majestic disdain—an operatic tenor about to be cuckolded.

She doesn't bother to watch. She merely waits, hands folded beneath her chin, as motionless as Cleopatra, until he is out of hearing.

Do I embarrass you? she asks, fixing Muhlbach with an undeniable gaze. You act sort of stiff. Sort of British. Did anybody ever tell you that? I'm not trying to sound critical because actually it appeals to me. Listen, have you got a piece of paper?

I'm afraid not.

Anything's okay.

A business card?

Great. And I need a pencil or a pen. I mean, if you want to call me.

Call you?

Yeh. Don't you want to?

Of course, he answers, reaching into his coat.

You don't sound like you mean it.

Yes. Yes indeed. I'd love to.

So all right, I'll give you my number.

When are you ordinarily at home?

I'm in and out, but you could call tonight around eleven.

Tonight?

Sure. Tonight's okay.

At that instant the betrayed lover arrives with cigarettes, just in time, perhaps, to have heard what was said.

Twenty minutes later, after putting away most of the duck à l'orange and whatever else she has found appetizing, Lambeth complains of a headache. She must go to the ladies' lounge for an aspirin.

Muhlbach and López rise from the table automatically, like two puppets on a stick, and wait until she departs. Then they sit down to continue eating. López, however, only picks at his food. He sips the wine. He prods the duck with the point of his knife. He sighs and coughs feebly into his napkin like an old man. His ebullience has seeped away, leaving him deflated, miserable, slumped in the chair with a lugubrious expression.

Well, thinks Muhlbach, it's too bad. She shouldn't have been so brutal. If she's decided to get rid of him, all right, I suppose that's her privilege. Or at least that's what happens in life. Love isn't always a perpetual flame. But she should have been more considerate, he looks like he's been shot. However, he must have been expecting it. He must have known it would end like this. Approximately like this. After all, how many middle-aged men could reasonably hope to hold the attention of a young woman as spectacular as she is? Not many. Not very many. So, looking at the situation objectively, maybe he ought to appreciate his good luck, even if it didn't last very long.

López emits another gloomy sigh. He mutters in Spanish.

Muhlbach stops eating long enough to wipe the grease from his chin. I ought to keep quiet, he thinks. After all, it's none of my business whether or not they break up. It's just that he looks ready to do away with himself.

Forgive me if I butt in. This isn't my affair, so to speak, but I can't help remembering something you said at the Christmas party. You remarked that a young girl could ruin a man before he realized what was happening.

True.

Well, I bring this up only because it strikes me as curious. Your remark indicates that you must have known, at least to some extent, what you were getting into.

I would not deny this. Also, I believe I have said that it is my practice to take advantages—no—'advantage.' To take advantage of the opportunities which afford themselves. In my opinion to do otherwise is foolish.

Then you aren't sorry?

Sorry? No. López collects himself enough to waggle an index finger. In the words of a certain wise man, it is what one does not do that one will regret. Claro?

Yes indeed.

I forget the name of the wise man.

Muhlbach resumes eating. It seems to him that everything tastes exceptionally good. The duck, the wild rice, the spinach, everything on the table. One doesn't expect to be served spinach in an expensive French restaurant but whoever prepared it certainly knew his business.

López, having picked up a breadcrumb, stares at it like an invalid.

What a shame, Muhlbach reflects while cutting himself another thick slice of duck. She's just about destroyed the man. I never saw anybody in such a state. Amazing! Oh, she's tired of him, no question about it. If he swore by the Holy Virgin of Guadeloupe that he was going to dive into the Hudson on the stroke of midnight she'd probably yawn.

After eating the breadcrumb, Lopez continues. It is, I

believe, not impossible to recapture the bird on the wing—if you understand what I'm saying. As I'm sure that you do. Forgive me. I seem at the moment to express myself with clumsiness because of the circumstances, in addition to the fact that I do not feel well. Chingado! What a night.

You express yourself perfectly. By the way, what does chingado mean?

This is not a word you will be able to use.

I might, but never mind. Now tell me something. Your adventure, or whatever it should be called—has it been worthwhile? You said something about it being no bed of roses.

That is correct, yes. Almost. I have said, if you will permit me to remind you, that it has been not altogether like that. Not altogether. In other words, you understand, not completamente. At the same time one does not overlook the opposite side of the coin. Perhaps it will be impossible to explain, but I will try. There are, in Spanish, what we call las chichas. As in English, there are many words, many expressions, to describe these things, eh? But I will tell you that with this girl they are so soft, so round, with these little pink tips. Aiee, que bonitas! Do you know what I am talking about?

I do. And so does everybody else in the neighborhood.

Excuse me, I'm sorry. It is not my wish to be indiscreet. You will have to pardon me. What I would like to explain to you, however, is that there are very many benefits to be had from this girl. Very many. Now you ask if to me this 'adventure' will have been worthwhile, or if, because perhaps the whole thing is ending, I regret what I have done. The answer is no. No! We are to enjoy the delightful fruit of the earth. Naturally you know to what I refer. We are to enjoy them, let me repeat, rather than to be afraid that possibly the juice will be—ah, what's the word? Agrio. How do you call agrio?

Agrio?

Let me think. I believe 'sower.' The juice of the lemon is sower.

Sour.

Thank you. Anyway that's not life, that's death. La muerte. Verdad? You understand?

Yes, and I agree.

No, you are different. It is your habit to be always cautious. Always, if I am not wrong, and I believe I am not, because I have watched. Yes, it is your habit to be careful, to take no chance. To be sure of what you are doing all the time. I congratulate you, but as for myself I could not live like that.

I don't necessarily consider myself cautious.

Permit me to disagree. On the contrary, yes. Yes, I would say so. Because I have watched you not only this evening while you are talking to Lambeth, but also, of course, on the other occasion when we met. You are like a person skating on thin ice, as the expression goes.

I suppose I'm not impetuous, but on the other hand I doubt if your use of the word 'cautious' could be justified. Not that it's important.

López shrugs. It's not important. Besides as you have said, this is not your affair.

Now what does that imply? Muhlbach wonders. Is he

hinting that I ought to keep my distance from Lambeth? He sounds a bit touchy, though I would be too. What a change since Christmas. She's sucked his blood, he's ready to collapse. He's still as dapper as a chipmunk, but the way he keeps plucking bits of lint from his coat—and he laughs rather frantically when he does laugh. And the way he slumps in the chair, as though he'd just swallowed poison. Well, whose fault is it? Getting involved with a girl half his age—I must say that's laying your head on the block. After all, what did he have to offer? Not much. If he was rich, all right, so long as both parties understood the situation—a willing buyer and a willing seller. But I suspect he dines at the automat more often than not. No, they don't belong together. Even under the best of circumstances there would be something inappropriate about the relationship. Then, too, I get the feeling she might not have recovered from the death of that flier. Yes, that should be considered.

After having refilled the wine glasses Muhlbach clears his throat.

Now granted this is none of my business, López, and if you prefer to talk about something else I'd be amenable. But your comment about recapturing the bird sticks in my mind. Do you honestly think you can? After all, Lambeth's an extraordinary creature. She must be deluged with proposals as well as propositions—not just from men our age who are much better equipped financially, but from quite a few handsome young musketeers.

Yes. She will be coming back from the ladies' room to say to me: 'Rafael, look, another telephone number.

What shall I do with it?' Oh, I understand, believe me, what you are saying. It's always the same, somebody is watching her every place we go. I know. I am not blind. Did I not see you outside the restaurant? And they have been watching this table, asking themselves how it will be possible to make the acquaintance of this girl, so now if you go to the lounge you will find somebody, maybe two of them, standing around smoking cigarettes just waiting for her. Eh? Go and look.

I'll take your word for it.

Es la vida, pero no me gusta.

You've lost me.

I was saying that's life, although one does not need to like it.

Ah, I see. Entiende.

No, that is not correct. One must say Entiendo in order to say I myself understand. Entiende is to say 'you' understand.

All right, I'll try to remember. But what I wanted to point out was that neither you nor I, nor any man of our generation, could be considered particularly attractive to a girl of Lambeth's age. Granted there are exceptions. Some of those movie stars, for instance. But in general you've got to agree.

No. Excuse me, I don't.

What can you offer a girl like that? If I may be so blunt.

López is not disconcerted. He taps the side of his head.

Muhlbach smiles thinly. You could be right, although I wouldn't bet on it.

I believe I am right, yes. We'll see, eh?

Something else has occurred to me. You do know that she was engaged.

To be married, yes. As sometimes it is the custom to say in this country: so what?

Have I offended you?

I would like very much to hear what you are going to tell me. You have not offended me, no. It is just that I have been asking myself why she takes so long. For one aspirin fifteen minutes. How long will it take to swallow one aspirin?

The question is rhetorical, of course, and Muhlbach helps himself to another piece of bread before continuing. What I was about to say was that she may not have gotten over the shock of her fiancé's death.

In my opinion, yes, you are wrong.

Suppose she hasn't.

Then there could be difficult complications if she is thinking about him. Naturally, as goes without saying. But I do not believe this is the case. On the contrary. I do not wish to sound boastful, however I have reason to believe she thinks very often of me. I am sure it will not be necessary to elaborate. I am sure that, as one man to another, you understand why I have reason to be of such an opinion.

Incredible, says Muhlbach to himself. The man's conceit is incredible. He's lost her but he won't admit it. The truth couldn't be more obvious.

Maybe you should divorce yourself from her, so to speak. Find somebody else, perhaps. I can see how that would be painful, but in the long run you might save yourself some additional pain. In other words, why not accept the fact that your little bird has flown and make the best of it?

No.

You were lucky to have her for a while. You were persistent, which is to your credit, and you were fortunate. I envy you. Any man would. But now, it would seem to me, the affair is ending. Let me put it this way. I've read someplace that we believe that according to our desire we're able to change the things around us—alter the facts, if you follow me, until they accord with our wishes. But this, of course, is a delusion. We can never change facts. What we can do, though, is to alter the shape of our desire. Does that make any kind of sense?

I am listening.

Well, what this amounts to is that once we've discovered something else to desire we find ourselves indifferent to whatever was tormenting us previously. Which is to say the situation we'd hoped to change because it was intolerable to us has now become more or less insignificant.

López appears to be meditating.

A few moments later the object of his passion and the root of his misery returns from the ladies' lounge. Two aspirin tablets have not helped. The headache is beastly.

Muhlbach expresses his regret. López, invariably diplomatic, acts solicitous. And Lambeth plays her part with consummate skill, touching her forehead, wrinkling her brow not too much, just enough. She is so sorry to break up the evening.

After they have wished him goodnight and walked away Muhlbach reaches for the wine bottle. This is preposterous—utterly preposterous! he murmurs, and then goes on talking to himself. Everybody knew what was happening. López is no fool. And she knew that he knew. We understood each other perfectly, yet all of us pretended. What a farce. And I took part in it. But what else could I have done? For that matter, what else could they have done? And now I've got her number in my pocket!

This, too, seems astonishing. He stares into the wine with a mistrustful expression.

If I were Somebody, he reflects. If I were an ambassador, let's say, or owned a chunk of midtown real estate, or had won the Nobel Prize for tinkering around with a microscope—then it would make sense. But I peddle insurance. That's no disgrace, of course, nevertheless it's a bit strange. I'm intelligent enough, and thoughtful, and not unperceptive. I try to respect and understand opinions I disagree with. Yes, I'd have to be considered tolerant. My manners may be a trifle bourgeois, possibly outdated by today's standards, but nobody could say I was uncouth. So I do have certain qualities. And most of us tend to underestimate ourselves. Hmm. Well, I won't be mistaken for Cary Grant, but on the other hand I suppose I do see why Lambeth might enjoy my company.

Still, it's odd. I remember when girls her age took a very natural interest in me—not that I was unbearably popular, but they did notice me, and some of them went out of their way to smile. Then I met Joyce and there were the children, and then her illness. Now all at once I'm halfway to wherever we're going and I can't begin to account for so many years. And the girls on the street these days don't quite see me. I might as well be a cardboard cutout. Oh, once in a while, yes, for an instant, but as soon as our eyes meet I know what they've decided. Well! I wonder if I should phone this girl. I suppose I should. It would be ridiculous not to.

Having wiped up the remnants of his duck and emptied the claret bottle Muhlbach now orders a cognac to accompany his after-dinner coffee. And presently it seems advisable to move to the bar, where he orders another cognac. Eleven o'clock, Lambeth said, so there's time enough. Besides, López might not have been evicted by eleven. He might hang around pleading his cause for quite a while, therefore it would be prudent to wait. Eleven-thirty ought to be about right.

But what will I say? he asks himself. Because I'm not going over there, if that's what she has in mind. And I suspect that's what she does have in mind. Not tonight I'm not. López may have been right, I'm more cautious than I like to admit. What's behind this sudden overture?

Warming the cognac between his palms, Muhlbach studies himself in the long smoky gold mirror and decides that the answer might be as simple as it seems: Lambeth, perhaps to her own surprise, has felt herself drawn to this mature well-tailored gentleman. Yes. A man of obvious refinement. Tactful. Cultivated. Discerning. One might even say discriminating. Genteel. Subtly humorous. Moderately prosperous. Sober—possibly too sober, a bit professorial. At any rate, why shouldn't she feel attracted to such a man? Certain men remain mysteriously vital throughout their lives. Look at Chevalier. Look at Rubens having affairs with models whose grandmothers he painted and seduced half a century earlier.

All the same, Muhlbach reflects, I just can't help being suspicious. I know what I want to believe, but I also know that I could be on the verge of doing something stupendously foolish. If she were thirty, let's say, instead of whatever she is—twenty, I think Eula said—in that case I wouldn't hesitate, I'd scratch on her door at the first opportunity. But the way things are I wonder if she might be trying to sell me a slice of the Brooklyn Bridge. So I think what I ought to do is invite the young lady out some evening. It might be wise to know a little more about her before committing myself. I'm not exactly a college kid who can afford to try anything once, I've got too much at stake. Otto and Donna, first of all. I don't intend to fritter away the money for their education. Nor lose their respect. Nor start anything that might generate rumors in the office. I certainly don't want Hammersmith peering over his spectacles at me. Besides it isn't as though I were starved for a woman—there's always Eula. Yes, there's always Eula. If only she didn't bore me. Well, that's not true because she isn't a bore. The truth is, she doesn't excite me. Thursday before last I had to pretend. I didn't want her to feel insulted. Though she may not have been deceived. Probably she wasn't. Well, so much for self-pity, the time's come—I've got to phone.

But upon consulting his watch Muhlbach is dumbfounded to learn that eleven and eleven-thirty have long since evaporated. It is now close to midnight. He is also surprised to discover that he is not particularly anxious to call Lambeth. How much more comfortable it would be to have another drink and simply imagine the conversation. In fact the thought of inviting her out—spending an entire evening talking to her—the whole idea has become vaguely repugnant.

What could we say to each other? he asks himself. Could we talk about our careers? What I know about modeling could be stuffed in a thimble, and I doubt if she'd care for a discourse on the pitfalls of corporate insurance. All right, what else have we? Music? I wonder if we'd enjoy the same sort. Somehow I doubt it. She wouldn't care for an evening of Boccherini and I—well, of course I can't predict her taste but I'm afraid it might run to jazz or perhaps those screaming androgynous freaks with electric guitars and platform shoes. As for art, if she's interested at all I expect she follows the trend, whatever gimmicks are in style this season—bent neon tubes or one dozen white vinyl horseshoes hanging in a row. I suppose I'm en retard. I don't suppose Rodin, Vermeer & Company can provide any fresh insights after so many years but at least they're genuine and I've had it up to the neck with mountebanks. All right, what else? Clothes? That discussion might last three minutes. Travel? Hardly. I seldom get past Newark and unless I'm very much mistaken she's seen even less of the world. Politics? Sports? Books? Been to any good movies lately? No, neither have I. What else? Precious little. Pretty soon we'd be ladling the silence like soup.

Also, there are a couple of things about that girl I just plain mistrust. Once or twice her voice took on an ugly edge. And her features can turn to ice. She could get quite nasty. And her color sense—I like muted tones. Ochre. Rust. Burnt orange. She obviously prefers the primaries. Then that habit of flinging her hair around like a Georgetown actress. Hmm . . .

Muhlbach scratches the end of his nose. He polishes his glasses. He looks again at his wristwatch. After a while he begins to improvise a little composition on the bar with his fingertips. At last, annoyed and puzzled that an almost accidental supper table flirtation seems to have become a noose, he slides off the stool with a bleak expression and goes in search of a telephone. With any luck she'll already be asleep. And if so, that should be the end of the affair.

But she is not asleep, she sounds wide awake. He asks if he has interrupted anything.

Like what? she replies. Give me a for instance.

Oh, let's see. For instance, Don Juan Rafael might be serenading you. 'La Paloma,' for instance.

He never got out of the elevator.

Why not?

I shut it in his face. As a matter of fact I shut the cage on his finger.

How cruel.

I'm sorry about his finger. I didn't mean to do that. But anyway he got furious. He started calling me these awful names.

I'd be furious, too.

Oh yeah?

Muhlbach realizes that he has been leaning away from the telephone. I don't want to talk to her, he thinks. I'm trying to be clever and amusing and it's a mistake. I don't know why I called. This is ridiculous. I should have thrown away her number and gone home and listened to records or watched television. Instead, like a prime jackass, I stuck my neck out.

Then, exasperated, he hears himself ask almost eagerly if they could get together some evening—perhaps next weekend.

After a long silence Lambeth agrees, although not with much tact:

Okay, I guess so. What have you got in mind?

How about a concert or a ballet? I'm not sure what's playing, but I did see an ad for some Spanish dance troupe.

That might be fun.

Wonderful, Lambeth. I'll look into the ticket situation tomorrow. Which evening would you prefer?

You name it.

Suppose we say Saturday because I'm sometimes delayed at the office on Friday. The show probably starts at eight but as soon as I get tickets I'll be in touch with you. And we might plan on supper afterwards.

Yeah, all right.

You sound indifferent.

No. No, that's okay, I'd like to go.

Well then, until Saturday . . .

And Muhlbach waits, expecting a social pleasantry, but without another word she hangs up.

TICKETS for the Spanish dancers are not easy to find but after having inquired at several agencies he obtains a pair in the second row.

When he reports to Lambeth that they will be almost on stage she responds as enthusiastically as a schoolgirl. And it seems to Muhlbach, seated at his desk, that she sounds much too young—closer to fifteen than twenty—and he swivels around in a narrow arc, frowning. Then it occurs to him that she has a younger sister.

Could this be a joke? Could she have put her sister on the line? If so, for what purpose? Yet the voice is hers, except for that peculiar euphoria. The intonation, the erratic rhythm, the deliberate huskiness. It must be Lambeth.

You won't mind being so close to the stage?

Hey, no! I'm really excited.

Well, good. I'm pleased. I wasn't sure if you actually wanted to go.

Sure! If I sounded cranky on the phone the other night I'm sorry.

That's quite all right. It was rather an awkward situation.

You can say that again!

Well! So everything's settled. You can expect me a few minutes after seven on Saturday. And if anything should come up in the meantime—that is, if for any reason you can't make it—you could reach me here at the office. I'll tell Gloria to put you through.

Now why in the world did I say that? he asks himself. I halfway invited her to cancel out. I suppose I'm afraid she will, though there's no reason she should. She called me Karl. At the restaurant it was Mr. Muhlbach. And she did sound excited, I believe she does want to go out with me. But do I want to see her? I can't make up my mind. It's like the taste of those sweet-sour dishes. I can't decide.

By the end of the week he finds it very difficult to concentrate on his work. He realizes that he is able to give the appearance of listening when someone speaks, that he comprehends what has been said, and that he can answer a question sensibly if unimaginatively. Yet it's as if I've been displaced, he thinks, evicted from my body. As though I were outside of myself. And he remembers that this is how he used to feel many years ago when he had been hypnotized by some adolescent Messalina in a cashmere sweater. It became impossible to pay attention to Civics or Latin. Nothering mattered except the relationship, which as a rule had existed only in his head.

I thought those days were over, he reflects while drawing still another meaningless geometrical design on the scratch pad. I thought I'd outgrown that kind of foolishness, but apparently not. Here I am dawdling around, wasting the afternoon, anticipating my Saturday night date. Anybody watching me would assume I was struggling with some important decision. Metropolitan's brilliant executive at work. Hah! My God, if Hammersmith could read my mind I'd be out of a job. But I suppose there's nothing to be alarmed about as long as I'm aware of the situation. I appear to be functioning. I don't believe anybody has noticed that I'm simply imitating myself. So as long as I don't do anything bizarre . . .

He blinks, leans forward in the swivel chair and reaches for the intercom:

Gloria, would you make sure that Mr. Hammersmith receives a copy of the Durstine memo?

I already took it up. You told me this morning.

Oh. Well, that's fine. Good. Now let's see, we have a conference in Howard's office at five?

Uh huh.

'Uh huh' instead of 'Yes, sir,' which means that the outer office must be empty.

Have I any appointments?

Miss Cunningham got here a couple of minutes ago.

Did you say Miss Cunningham? Eula?

Right. She says she doesn't need an appointment. Oh . . . uh . . . Gloria continues after a pause. She's mad at me, I guess. She said she wanted to surprise you. Anyway she just started down the hall so she ought to be there about now.

At that moment the door opens and Eula sweeps in, dressed for an ostrich fair.

Dear boy! she cries, placing a lavender pastry box on the blotter. Happy Birthday!

Muhlbach, standing up, attempts to look pleasantly surprised.

Ah ha! Hello! I haven't seen you for some time, Eula.

And whose fault would that be? Now open your present. I know perfectly well your birthday isn't until September but I was out shopping and happened to pass this marvelous little bakery and I thought, oh, why not! So I did. They're delicious. Delicious!

Inside the box, each nestled in a fluted paper crib, lie one dozen chocolate éclairs.

Eula, pulling off her gloves, has not stopped talking. She discovered the nicest drapes at Bloomingdale's—a floral pattern. The old drapes had become impossible. Marlene and the girls were over for bridge last Tuesday—no, it must have been Monday because the hairdresser's father-in-law was suddenly taken sick—and Marlene made a point of staring at the drapes, which is so typical of her. At any rate, Eula continues, sinking into a chair, when I saw that ad from Bloomingdale's I simply jumped. Now they should be delivered tomorrow so I want you to come for supper. Will you?

Tomorrow? No, I'm afraid I can't, Eula. I've already made plans.

You despicable man! I don't know why I put up with you. Would Gloria like an eclair?

I'll ask. She thought you were peeved at her.

How could I be! That sweet child—though you really should tell her to stop chewing gum.

Gloria, who seldom needs to be coaxed toward anything edible, responds in her most sophisticated Brooklyn voice that she will be there as soon as she can find her shoes.

And not long after her arrival two more secretaries appear hungrily at the door. Evidently the word has spread.

When the party is over Muhlbach finds himself unable to get back to work. This always happens after a visit from Eula. Not that she makes an effort to disrupt—well, yes, she does. Yes, he thinks, rolling a pencil between his palms, as a matter of fact that's precisely what she does do. She interrupts on purpose. She seems to feel I'm strapped to a treadmill, which is true, and therefore I should be grateful for a break in the routine—which is not true. I'll never understand that woman. For the life of me I couldn't waltz into somebody's office with a pasteboard box full of eclairs. I wish I could—what an experience. Maybe I should try it. Yes, try a stunt like that on Hammersmith. He'd have me in Bellevue. But it all comes naturally to Eula. Of course she's mad as a spring hare. Once in a while I suspect she actually is a bit demented, then she pulls another of those stock market maneuvers twenty-four hours ahead of the crowd. Incredible! She has some kind of supernatural instinct. She must have made a young fortune on that Enovid investment. I kept saying it was speculative. Much too speculative, I said. But oh no, she had a hunch. I can't explain it, Karl, I simply have this overwhelming hunch. All right, I said, it's your money, just remember that I warned you. Good God, the time I've spent studying the market—charts, seminars, bulletins, newsletters—all for what? Eula gets a 'hunch' and makes as much in five days as Rockefeller. There's got to be an explanation. But in any event I wish she'd stop interrupting me at work. I wish she'd settle her affections on somebody else. Whatever I felt for her at the beginning seems to have dried up. I don't know why. She hasn't changed much so it must be my fault. Although it's partly her neck. That always troubled me, even at first, but I was able to ignore it. Now for some incomprehensible reason all I can think about is what a short neck she has. Well, whatever the cause, whether it's the brevity of Eula's neck or my advanced age or something else, I wish she'd stop bestowing her favors on me. She's a good woman and she's fond of me—more than that—she's in love with me, I suppose. But I can't seem to reciprocate. If she looked like Lambeth, for example, or let's say an elder sister of Lambeth—yes, that would solve the problem.

Then he begins to think about Lambeth, and the idea of actually spending an evening with her seems improbable. It won't happen. It might conceivably happen, but the likelihood is that it won't. She'll break the date, maybe at the last instant.

Saturday morning, stretched out on the chaise in the garden, mildly stupefied by the monotonous cheep of sparrows and a patronizing April sun, holding a book on his lap to disguise the fact that he is doing nothing, Muhlbach anticipates the telephone. Sooner or later it will ring. Mrs. Grunthe, displeased by the noise, will answer. The kitchen door will open and with ponderous unconcern she will deliver the news. Lambeth has called to say that her mother has been electrocuted. Or the sky is falling. Or she's gotten a modeling assignment in Bangkok and must leave at once.

Then the phone does ring. Muhlbach shuts his eyes.

Mrs. Grunthe, however, instead of stepping outside, hangs up the receiver, mutters something unfavorable and plods off in a different direction to resume her duties.

With his eyes closed he begins to wonder what Lambeth's apartment will be like. Orderly or chaotic? Sterile or hospitable? Will she have a cat? A parakeet? An aquarium? What sort of books and records? How has she decorated the walls? And will the furniture be expensive Danish modern, for instance, or thrift shop salvage? In any case it should be enlightening because women supposedly reveal their true nature, much more so than men, by the interior of their rooms.

Yes, I'll pay attention, he thinks. I'll take some notes. But no matter what the place tells me I suspect I may be in for a surprise or two. I get the feeling she's like those Russian Easter eggs, smaller and smaller and smaller until—until what?

From the looks of the apartment she might as well be in a Bleecker street walk-up. Apple boxes, bricks and boards, a candle stuck in a wine bottle, repainted chairs, a tatami mat on the bare floor. On the walls a cheap Miro print, a Tantra poster, Humphrey Bogart as big as life, half a dozen tissue paper collages. Scandinavian crystal knickknacks litter the table like cut-glass doorknobs or fragments from a shattered cathedral window. Of animals, birds, or fish she has none, not so much as a guppy—except one thoroughly dead blowfish dangling from the ceiling on a string, no doubt a memento of some vacation. What else? A few dusty plants struggle against the hostile atmosphere. So! None of it is startling, only a little disconcerting. Disappointing, perhaps. There is a sense of dirtiness, of unemptied garbage in the kitchen and unwashed clothing thrown into the closet. The only genuine surprise is a trunk—an ancient steamer trunk, cracked and warped, with brass bands holding it in one piece and a hinged lock big enough for a bank vault. Where did she find it? Why does she have it? And Muhlbach, contemplating this trunk while he waits for her to emerge from the bedroom, reflects that she could toss all of her possessions except the plants into this relic and be gone in twenty minutes.

Her library consists mostly of paperbacks. Apparently she regards Rod McKuen as America's most significant poet, Allen Ginsberg running second. And what other intellectual nourishment have we? Henry Miller. William Burroughs. Tolkien. *The Well of Loneliness.* Organic food. Several books on drugs. Astrology. Yes, I did predict that, he tells himself. Now what else? A picture book about Marilyn Monroe. Scientology. *I Ching.* M. C. Escher prints. One of Heyerdahl's raft trips. A best seller by a formidable lady with three names.

Musically? She neglects her records, many of which are scattered about on the floor unprotected. Nothing classical in sight. Folk singers, rock bands . . .

Gazing at the immature shaggy faces that decorate these albums, bemused by their peculiar emptiness, it occurs to him that he does not recognize any of the names. Not a single one. He is as ignorant of these contemporary musicians as Lambeth must be of the great composers. Then he notices a pile of photographs. Presumably it would be all right to look through them. They are ballet photos and they have the glossy commercial appearance of publicity pictures.

Just then Lambeth emerges from the bedroom wearing gold sandals and the top half of what could be a pair of lime green pajamas. In an effort to avoid staring at her legs he tries to focus on a strand of pearls, probably imitation, which she has twisted around the lacquered pagoda on top of her head. The pearls, authentic or not, create a dazzling Renaissance effect vaguely reminiscent of some Florentine portrait. She is, to say the least, visible. Or, he thinks, to put it another way, she's astounding. Or outrageous. I wonder if we'll be arrested.

He decides to say nothing controversial about the dress—because she does seem to regard it as a dress and therefore suitable to wear in public. If I knew her better, he tells himself, I'd have the nerve to suggest something a trifle less flamboyant. The pearls, though, I do like that arrangement. It's absolutely wild but she manages to get away with it. And I could accept those Coney Island sandals provided she wore something conservative in between. A plain dress without much color would emphasize her features. Why does she cheapen herself with that preposterous green nightshirt? She looks like a high-priced hooker. Well, I've just got to pretend nothing's wrong. My God, it'll be a long time before I forget this date.

He holds up a ballet picture.

You?

Lambeth, tilting her head in order to attach a gold bangle to one ear, nods briefly.

It was taken in Buffalo the year before last while we were doing *Petrouchka.*

I had no idea you were a dancer. Somebody at that Christmas party told me you were studying dramatics. At City College, as I recall.

I was, but it got to be a drag.

So ballet is your forte?

Not anymore. I quit.

Muhlbach studies the photograph again. Might I ask why?

Laziness.

I don't believe that. Tell me the truth.

I told you.

If you insist. Now I'm not much of a judge, Lambeth, but on the basis of this picture I'd say you must have been pretty good.

Not good, not bad. Pas mal, my teacher used to say.

How long did you study?

Eight years.

And after eight years you simply dropped it?

I turned into a vegetable after Boyd got killed. I couldn't do a thing. I drank a lot. I didn't care what happened to me. And I met this older woman and started living with her. It was just terrible—I mean everything. Really, I couldn't begin to tell you. I used to turn on the gas sometimes and lie there listening to it and wonder if I should shut the window. I almost did.

Do you still think about it? I mean suicide.

No. I get real depressed once in a while. Like I yell and throw stuff. But except for that I'm okay.

Muhlbach returns to the photograph. You look altogether professional. I very nearly didn't recognize you.

Lambeth picks up a picture of three girls in black leotards at the exercise bar. That's me in the middle.

Not much of the dancer's face can be seen, but the line of the cheek and the lithe proportions of the body—yes, that would be Lambeth. Transfixed on a sheet of glossy paper how elegant she is. How poised, how infinitely sophisticated and how innocently lovely.

Muhlbach asks if he might have a print of it.

Wouldn't you rather have one on stage? I mean, you could have the *Petrouchka.*

No. No, I want this.

You really like it?

Beyond words.

She glances at the picture curiously, yet with disdain. All she sees is herself stretching at the exercise bar.

Okay, it's yours. Hey, do you want a collage? I make them.

Do you? I thought so.

He turns around to look at them pinned to the wall, beyond doubt the work of an amateur. They are totally uninteresting. But while he is contemplating them as seriously as possible so that her feelings will not be hurt, leaning down a little to give the impression that he wants to inspect them closely, he begins to feel touched by these meaningless arrangements of colored paper. It is not that they are amateurish, they are childish. No, not childish. Childlike would be more accurate. As though she were a child cutting and pasting scraps of tissue paper. The idea is almost unbearable.

Do you want one? she asks with radiant eyes.

Yes, Muhlbach answers, wondering if she will sense the lie. Yes, I should say I do.

Honest?

They're charming.

Pick out whichever one you like best.

Would you make one especially for me?

Okay, sure. Except I don't think I could get around to it right away because I'm kind of busy. I mean I've got these modeling assignments.

That's all right, take your time. But I'll look forward to it. And now maybe we'd better start for the theater.

Lambeth goes off to get her coat.

The coat turns out to be a watery white item which comes down almost to her muscular knees and somehow manages to suggest that she is wearing nothing underneath, but at least it does conceal eight inches of thigh.

As they leave the apartment she gives his arm a definite squeeze. Muhlbach acknowledges the gesture with a tentative smile, then he begins talking about the show. He hopes she will enjoy it. There was a generally favorable review in yesterday's paper. And he goes on to say that he does not know much about Spanish dancing, having been to only one performance. He and his wife went to see the Carmen Amaya troupe some years ago.

You must have been married a long time.

Yes, he replies, nodding. And I was very happy. So was Joyce, I think. In fact I know she was. We were very close, Lambeth. I doubt if I could ever again feel that close to a woman. It's hard to explain.

No, I can dig it. I mean, like with me there could never be anybody except Boyd. So when like I got this telegram—well, I freaked.

We may need an interpreter, Muhlbach thinks. And aside from that, what are we going to talk about for the next several hours? The show, of course. And her ballet training—I'll get some good mileage there. And the apartment, I suppose. We can discuss Miro and Humphrey Bogart and Thor Heyerdahl and that antique trunk and whatever else I can remember. But this just may be one of the longest evenings of my life.

I was noticing those Scandinavian crystal knickknacks, he begins when the first silence falls. Were they a gift? Or are you something of a collector?

Mind your own business, she responds in a humorless voice. Never mind where I got those things, okay? I don't bug you so don't you bug me.

Muhlbach, too astonished to answer, looks straight ahead. She's stupid, he thinks. Good God, I didn't realize until this instant how stupid she is. I must have been blinded by that face.

In the taxi he reaches for her hand. Lambeth, I was only trying to make conversation. I didn't mean to irritate you. If I did, I'm sorry.

So forget it, she replies without much grace. But a moment later she relents. Hey, I don't want to jump up and down on you. Let's have a good time tonight.

I hope we will.

It's just if you expect to score points with me you better learn the rules, that's all.

Muhlbach carefully removes his hand. This is absurd, he tells himself. Utterly absurd. I don't know how I got myself into this. I've already been forced into the position of apologizing for something that wasn't my fault. A long evening—hah! I should say so. What I wouldn't give to be home right now. Even the sight of Mrs. Grunthe would be a relief.

And then, possibly constricted by the argument, his heart starts to thump irregularly. He listens to the rapid clumsy bumping while a light cold sweat collects on his forehead and a not unfamiliar fear climbs in his throat. This time it could happen. The intense tragic one-act drama which he has staged so many times in his mind now plays itself out with terrible force. It's like a fish, he thinks, turning away from Lambeth in order to cup one hand over his heart. That flopping—it's like a fish pulled out of the water.

He waits for the searing pain which is supposed to follow, but nothing happens. Then he becomes aware that one of Lambeth's hands is resting on his sleeve.

Are you all right?

Yes. Yes, of course, he answers, looking down with a sense of astonishment at the elegant white hand. That he could be seated in a taxi beside her seems unreal.

I'm fine. Yes, I'm fine. Why do you ask?

Because you—oh, I don't know. I was worried. I mean, you acted real weird.

By the time they arrive at the theater she has forgotten not only her concern but her anger. She clings to him as though they were bride and groom, and while getting settled in the second row she contrives to massage his leg. Muhlbach ignores the signal; nothing would be accomplished by any sort of response and it's hard to guess when or why or how she will erupt.

He opens the program. Together they look through it.

The principal dancer, Antonio de Triana, appears to be a small ferocious man with absolutely no hips and a carnivorous expression. He has been formally decorated by the Spanish government. The *Cruz de Caballero del Merito Civil* was bestowed upon him in recognition of his worldwide contribution to the cultural arts of Spain. Even as a child, according to the extravagant notes, his prodigious talent was observed and soon he was brought to public attention by the famous Argentinita. Before long he had been acknowledged as a unique artist whose body and soul combined effortless technique with the uninhibited masculine passion which so vividly exemplifies Spanish dancing. Dominant, yet never arrogant, Antonio de Triana heads what may be the finest company of artists ever assembled for a tour of the United States.

Maribel Granados, born in Algeciras, comes from a family of celebrated dancers. At the age of thirteen she appeared as soloist with Imperio Hurtado and later with Pacita Cintron. World renowned by the age of twenty, she often has been called the greatest living interpreter of the dances of Cádiz.

Pepe Moreno, a native of Seville, makes his American debut with Antonio, although he has long been known and applauded throughout the capital cities of Europe for his fiery presentation of flamenco dances.

Lydia Ortiz. Martin Astigarraga. Luis Granados—Maribel's brother. Felix Vargas. Gitanilla del Mar. Teresita Montoya. Each of these artists, if one may believe the program, is incomparable.

The first number, *Danza de Sitges,* portrays a flirtatious peasant lad pressing his advances upon two village maidens. However he soon learns that they are a match for him. *Nocturno,* the second number, will be a poetic dance inspired by the great Albeniz. Next comes *El Encantador,* a brief and tragic love affair made famous by Antonio. *Cana y Petenera,* in which a wicked courtesan finally meets a lover who dominates her and leads her to Hades, escorted by the spectres of her past conquests. *El Cortijo,* whose dynamic rhythms depict Spanish horsemen on the open plains. *Los Amantes de Valladolid. El Tecolete. Fantasia. Galician Suite. Soleares. Jota. Bulerias. La Molinera . . .*

It sounds like a full evening.

Antonio, that crafty performer, does not reveal himself in the opening number, nor in the second; but when at last he struts into view—traditional crisp flat black hat tilted over his cruel gypsy features, neck arched like a peacock, arms lifted, angrily snapping those bony fingers with a noise like pistol shots—the audience explodes. Applause, however, cannot seduce Antonio. He ignores the unctuous public. Like a spiraling hawk he circles Maribel Granados. All at once he gives a little jump and stamps his feet.

Muhlbach observes that Lambeth is gazing across the footlights with stunned admiration. Antonio has devoured her heart. Pepe Moreno, Luis Granados, Martin Astigarraga, Felix Vargas—none of these caballeros, no matter how virile or exciting, can hold her attention very long. If Antonio isn't on stage she wilts.

In the lobby during intermission she talks enthusiastically about almost all of the performers. She has been impressed by the emotional latitude of Teresita Montoya, by the dominant line of Astigarraga. Obviously she is familiar with Spanish dancing. She brings up celebrated names: Greco, Piquer, Tomas, Pilar Lopez.

All right, but what about Antonio?

She begins to caricature Antonio. She mocks the conceited lift of his head, the imperious step. She pulls down her eyebrows. She hurls a thunderbolt of smouldering gypsy contempt at the patrons in the lobby. And without quite leaping into the air she manages to imitate his furious insinuating hop, landing on her heels with a quick barrage of sound. But then, displeased, she stops. All at once she murmurs that she is going to the ladies' room.

A few seconds later Muhlbach finds himself face to face with A. Telemann Veach, he of the rancid breath and scarlet vest and abominable manners. He looks even more elephantine than he did at the party, and he is just as unceremonious.

Muhlbach! he growls with what might be construed as affection. How the Christ are you! Still pushing those two-bit stocks? Meet Nora Geller.

Nora Geller is not much bigger than a midget. Beneath a cloche hat, with an impossibly long cigarette holder and blood-red Cupid lips, she resembles Clara Bow. She smiles an engaging gap-toothed smile.

I am not his mistress, I am his agent, she chirps. How do you do, Mr. Muhlbach? I like that suit. Who does your tailoring?

Veach gives a snort. Been trying to hump this little broad for years. Lot of good it's done.

Ignore him, Mr. Muhlbach. He becomes gross whenever his wit fails. It's a pleasure to make your acquaintance. You're associated with Dean Witter, I understand. Or is it Shearson Hammil?

Neither. I'm not a stockbroker.

Veach grumbles and strokes his beard. Aw, come on. You were pitching some kind of snake oil.

You asked me about a company called Taggo.

Taggo! That's right. Now I got it—you peddle insurance. Prudential.

Metropolitan Mutual. But that's neither here nor there. We discussed other things than stocks and insurance. Hazlitt, for intance. And music. We talked about various composers. Grillparzer. Lully . . .

Veach isn't paying attention; he appears to be searching the crowd. All at once Muhlbach understands that he is trying to locate Lambeth.

I don't recall meeting you at the party, says Nora Geller.

Were you there?

I had to leave early, she replies, grinning through a veil of perfumed cigarette smoke.

Chasing some—Veach pauses long enough to belch—wop fag interior decorator, that's why she left. Christ what an awful party. Bootlickers, fairies offering to let me read their sonnets, scrawny old dames you wouldn't poke with a stick. I don't know why I went.

He adores parties, says Nora Geller. He finds scads of people to insult.

Veach grunts, tugs at his crotch, glares around the room.

You're in public, Nora murmurs, smiling with her upper lip.

Veach fixes her with his steady blue eye. If I wanted a Jewish mama I'd have had one. Then he turns to Muhlbach. What brought you here? You like this spick stuff?

Hypnotized by the malevolent eye, knowing it would be better to dodge the question, Muhlbach listens to himself explain about seeing Lambeth for the first time on the bus, arriving at the party together, seeing her again at La Galette, and deciding that because of her ballet training she might enjoy this show. By the way, he goes on, have you met her?

You schmuck! Veach grumbles. The little mink went home with me.

Nora gives a tiny scream. Oh! Isn't he dreadful? If he didn't earn so much money I'd drop him. Just pretend you don't hear what he says. He loves to play games with people. I should have warned you.

I'm aware of that, Muhlbach answers, conscious that both of them are studying him. However your client doesn't embarrass me. I've not forgotten our conversation during the holidays, nor his determination to flabbergast everybody he meets. I understand, too, that as a novelist he's professionally interested in my reaction. So your comment about playing games strikes me as rather appropriate.

Nora, me girl, Veach mutters with an affected Irish accent, did ye hear that? Did ye hear the man? Now who does the man sound like? Aw, he continues in his midwestern American voice, I dunno. Could be Oliver Wendell Holmes. Say something else, Muhlbach.

Not just now.

You squizzle the kid?

What?

You can tell me and Nora. You get in the kid's pants?

Enough is enough, Clara Bow protests, reaching up to place a miniature hand on his blubbery arm. You've made our friend uncomfortable.

Veach chuckles, leaning on the cane. Spit it out, Muhlbach. We're pals. You can trust me. Let's hear the bloody details.

I believe you're making a considerable assumption.

You hear him, Nora? Considerable assumption. Keep talking, Muhlbach.

Nora Geller pretends to sigh. She waves her eyelashes. He regards you as an anachronism, Mr. Muhlbach. You fascinate him. Do you feel flattered? You should.

I can't honestly say that I do. However I have a question which you, as his agent, might be able to answer. If I am to be the prototype for a character in one of his novels do I share in the royalties?

Aw, Veach complains, mopping his beefy purplish face with a handkerchief. Christ, everybody wants a piece. Ten percent to this greedy broad. Three wives drinking my blood. What a hell of a note. You think I work at the mint? Let's get back to the subject.

I'd rather not. I don't care to be prodded into a discussion of Lambeth. As a matter of fact I resent your inquisitiveness.

Why don't they pump some air through this dump? Veach asks, stuffing the handkerchief into his hip pocket. Listen, Muhlbach, you want to know how many times I topped the kid?

Oh! exclaims Nora. Such a disgusting person! Why I put up with him I'll never know.

Veach ignores her. Once, Muhlbach. One time.

I don't exist, says Nora, tapping ashes on the carpet. I am not here, I am somewhere else. Tonight I am in Venice. I love Venice.

Veach pokes Muhlbach in the stomach with an arthritic nicotine-soaked finger. That's all you're gonna get, pal, just what I got—one roll. Old goats like us, she puts out the welcome mat one time. Why? Veach lifts his massive fat shoulders and breathes heavily. I don't know, I can't even guess. Hell, sure I can guess, anybody could. That's not the point. One squirt, Roscoe, then out you go ass over teakettle. You think I'm still playing games. Well, you wait. Because your luck ain't gonna be no better than mine or anybody else's, including that little jack-in-the-box from Honduras.

Muhlbach turns to the agent, who immediately looks up at him with an expression of despair which may or may not be contrived.

Miss Geller, I have a question. In the event I decide to read one of your client's romances, which would you recommend?

Veach waves her silent. Don't make jokes, Muhlbach. Listen to me. That kid's sick as a shithouse owl. You chase her around the mulberry bush and they'll be picking you up with a stick and a spoon. I know what I'm talking about. You don't believe me? Why won't you believe me? Then he goes on, wagging his head sorrowfully: You can't see any further than a bull in a stockyard. You're hooked worse than I was, you poor bastard. Tell him, Nora.

Mr. Muhlbach, you're hooked worse than he was, you poor bastard.

Veach groans. He leans on his cane. Holy Mary! Two comedians!

Miss Geller, do you happen to be acquainted with Lambeth?

Fortunately, no. Although I've seen her.

Why do you say 'fortunately'?

Please don't ask.

But you do know what she looks like?

Nora Geller nods uncertainly. Beneath the cloche her huge brown eyes register alarm while she waits for the next question.

What's your opinion? Or let me put it this way: how would you describe her? No, that's not quite what I mean. What I want to find out is what you think of her.

I sympathize.

You what? You 'sympathize'?

I'm not the person to ask. I detest gorgeous girls.

Veach interrupts. She told you she was a model, I bet. Rick somebody and all that crap. Tomorrow she'll get the big break. Sure, sure. Listen, Muhlbach, the kid's a loser. I've seen thousands of them. And if you don't cut loose she'll take you down with her—down so far nobody's even going to hear the splash.

Have you any more advice?

You snap your fingers at advice so I'll give you facts. She got busted for shoplifting last summer. She served ninety days and if she was a frump or a ghetto kid she'd still be cooling her twat in the can. Now you better pay attention, brother, I'm doing my best to help you. Have you met Angelo? Nope, not yet. I can tell. Lieutenant Angelo di Prima—one of our finest. He looks like a baboon with smallpox and he'd as soon kick you in the nuts as shake hands. I figured you might have met him because the dumb broad gets a bang out of introducing her studs.

I look forward to meeting the lieutenant.

He could drop in on you one rainy day.

For what reason?

Because he's jealous, that's what reason. Also, he's a maniac. Don't get salty with him, Muhlbach. Honest to God, I've started to worry about you. You jumped precincts and you don't know as much as Little Red Riding Hood. Angelo is wild about her. He brings her spumoni and marzipan and wants her to meet his mama. He's on the vice squad and she'd have been yanked off the streets a long time ago—about the age of twelve—if it wasn't for that pasta-loving assassin.

Now Mr. Muhlbach, says Nora Geller, tugging at his sleeve, promise you won't believe everything you hear. Promise?

Should I believe any of it?

Just then the house lights flicker.

Oh! she exclaims. I'm so glad. I thought this intermission would never end.

Veach chuckles. Let me know if you want to hear more, you poor schlemiel. Anytime. Just say the word and I'll give you the number of a quack in the Village who helped her out when she was sweet fifteen. And there's a Barbados nigger by the name of Cedric who can tell stories about your date that'd make you lose your lunch. Don't believe a word, do you? Hell no, you don't! I can read your face like a circus poster. Tell the man what a schlemiel he is, Nora.

Right!

Attagirl, says Veach, patting her on the back. Now let's go watch those faggoty spick dancers.

No sooner has Veach lumbered out of sight than Lambeth returns.

Why did you avoid him? Muhlbach asks while they walk down the aisle.

What a dumb question, she answers. That's really dumb! And then for a few steps she becomes a vicious caricature—walking with difficulty, depending on a nonexistent cane, her cheeks full of air, her perfect unblemished face an inexplicably twisted disagreeable mask.

During the rest of the performance Muhlbach slumps in his chair with a thoughtful expression. In all probability Veach was lying, manufacturing scandal. Or at most he might have been embellishing a few stale rumors—of which there were more than enough at the party. Yes, that must be it. Anything to get a rise out of me, but he failed. I handled the situation pretty well, which I don't always do. Of course there could be a grain or so of truth in what he said, I'm not as naïve as he assumes I am. I'll keep my eyes open. But on the whole I'm sure he was fabricating—playing his usual game. It's just possible he tried to get a date with her and she turned him down. That would explain a lot.

At last the show concludes—the castanets and staccato boots and meticulous guitars, the muscular thighs and whirling black locks and sinuous provocative story-telling hands, the incessant dry butterpat clap, the hoarse frantic Mediterranean tales of revenge, passion and ineffable grief. It would seem that these baroque Spaniards must have exhausted the emotions of the audience, to say nothing of their own; but suddenly Antonio strides from the wings, dripping perspiration, almost hidden by an armload of red roses. As confidently as a prize stallion he steps to the front of the stage and begins tossing roses to the ladies. He does not discriminate. Young or old, thin or fat, ugly or pretty—any woman will do. It is, of course, a show business trick.

But then with insuperable conceit, not once masking his furious eyes, he struts across the proscenium toward Lambeth. And having kissed the last rose he pitches it into her lap. Her cheeks turn brighter than a day in spring. She has difficulty breathing. People in the balcony stand up in order to see her. Everybody in the audience wants a look at Antonio's favorite.

On the way out of the theater Lambeth presses the magic rose to her breast. She is either unwilling or unable to speak, and the pupils of her eyes are so dilated that she can hardly see where she is going. All of which is a bit remarkable—considering how she mocked him.

While waiting for her to return from paradise Muhlbach asks himself if he feels jealous of Antonio. Well, yes. But on the other hand, no, because Antonio can't be considered a rival. She obviously is mad about him, a blind man could see that much, but she'll never meet him. Never? Not tonight, at least. And a few days from now he and his turbulent lieutenants will be devastating the better half of Boston or Detroit or some other provincial capital. Given a week, perhaps, he might somehow contrive to locate Lambeth and would then need all of three minutes to seduce her. Fortunately he won't be in the neighborhood that long.

However, Muhlbach continues to himself, if I enjoy turning myself inside out with jealousy I should have plenty of opportunities because every time I look around some idiot seems to be gawking at her.

Oh! Lambeth exclaims during supper, and she opens her purse. Here. This is for you. She holds out a business card.

Embossed on the card is the name Otis E. Kraft, which sounds like an anagram. Mr. Kraft is an architect. Lambeth explains that this terribly handsome aggressive man caught up with her on the way to the ladies' room and insisted that she accept his card. She can't imagine why.

He expects you to call. You know that perfectly well.

Should I?

Why have you brought this up? Muhlbach asks after thinking about it. What's the point? Am I supposed to become enraged?

Lambeth shrugs. He wanted me to split.

Do you mean leave the show?

He told me to get my coat, she answers as though explaining something to a child, and wait for him on the corner.

What did you say?

I'm still here.

Yes, but for how long? Muhlbach wonders.

So I see, he remarks aloud, more irritably than he had intended. Now what should I do with the gentleman's card?

Oh, don't be such a drag. I mean really! And I'll tell you what else he said, she continues a few minutes later. He invited me to go to Mexico. He said he'd take me to

Puerto Vallarta. I told him I couldn't, but maybe I should've said yes. It sure would be more fun than spending an evening with you.

Muhlbach looks at her with surprise because, until that brief contretemps over the card, she had seemed to be enjoying herself.

Anyhow I've already been there, she goes on in a petulant voice. That's where I spent February. It was fabulous—just fabulous! I love Puerto Vallarta. The Burtons were there and Dick is an absolute riot. Liz can be a charmer too, only you know how temperamental she is. And of course she's put on weight. I told her right in front of everybody that she ought to lose thirty pounds and you should have seen her expression. I mean, it really was something!

Muhlbach, gazing at her through the candlelight, reflects that she looks a trifle unreal, like a mannequin. Or a remarkably lifelike portrait by John Singer Sargent—the daughter of Madame X, perhaps, home from an elite finishing school. A pampered young lady, self-indulgent, impatient, rude to the servants. Yet at the same time there is something oddly degenerate about her. Licentious. Very nearly depraved. Those wide pink lips and the slightly greasy blue eyelids. The high thin arrogantly arched brows. This is the face of a deeply sensual woman.

What's the matter? she demands. Why are you staring at me? Don't you think I know the Burtons?

Of course not. You're making this up.

Am I?

Every word.

And just who the hell are you? she asks with sullen

contempt. What do you know about me? You just met me. You sit there like that and tell me I didn't go to Puerto Vallarta. You've never been there either. So all right, I didn't! So what? So I went to Miami Beach last month, at least I got out of the city, which is more than you did. All you do is go back and forth and back and forth like ten million other little slaves.

Nor is she through. She has a few more things to say on the subject. Muhlbach listens with the best face he can put on, hoping to appear understanding and interested and sympathetic.

Okay, she remarks at last, satisfied that she has established her position. Okay, so I went to Miami Beach with this fat old repulsive jerk from the garment district because he told me he knew a lot of bigshots and we could stay at the Fountainebleau in this private penthouse. You know where we stayed? At the south end of the beach where there's—I mean nobody! I just couldn't believe it. Which shows how dumb I am, because all he wanted was to get laid. I thought I was going to throw up every time he put his hands on me. And this is the honest truth—he asked me to call him Izzy. Oh hey, listen! I didn't plan to drop all that on you. I don't know what got into me, I sort of got started and —hey, forgive me? Please? She reaches across the table to squeeze his hand.

All right. Let's change the subject.

Forgive?

Yes.

Honest?

Yes yes yes yes.

Okay. Listen, can I ask a favor? Here's what I was

thinking. I was wondering if, after we get better acquainted, maybe you'd invite me someplace. Like maybe we could take a real trip together.

Her crystalline eyes are expressionless. Her usually suggestive lips reveal nothing. Is she joking? Probably. If not, what would she want in exchange? What would be the price of a weekend with her? Or a week or two? How many promissory notes sooner or later would turn up? And in what disguise?

Suppose we did, he replies with a faint smile. Where would you like to go?

She answers at once: The Riviera! Monaco and St. Tropez and the whole bit. Wouldn't that be fun? We could visit the Prince.

Is he a friend of yours?

We've known each other for ages!

Have you indeed?

Oh yes. I adore the Prince. Grace, too. She's sweet.

All right, suppose we do up the Riviera. Then what?

Now it's your turn.

Let me think. Patmos. Next stop, Patmos.

Hey, where's that? I never heard of it. What did you call it?

Patmos. It's one of the Dodecanese Islands, which means there should be twelve of them—though according to the encyclopedia there are thirteen. Isn't that strange?

Karl, you're nuts. Why do you want to go to Patmos?

I understand there's a library in a monastery on the highest peak of the island which has the oldest books in the world. I read about it when I was a child. One of those books dates from the fourth century. And they have illuminated manuscripts from the Middle Ages. Wouldn't that be interesting? We could spend an afternoon in the library drinking ouzo and thumbing through the oldest books in the world.

You really are. I mean a lot of people try to act nuts but, man, you are!

And from Patmos, Lambeth, we could jump aboard a pirate boat for Turkey. How does that sound?

I like you, she replies after a moment, and begins toying with her necklace. You're different from most of the men I meet. I hope we get to know each other better. Hey, do they still have pirates in Turkey?

Yes indeed, says Muhlbach after emptying his wine glass. They have long mustaches and shaved heads and they all wear baggy pantaloons and red slippers with pointed toes. They're dreadful men. Dreadful! They'll try to make off with you.

Will you let them?

Never!

What will we do?

We'll escape in the nick of time.

And after we've escaped from the pirates where will we go?

Now it's your turn.

No, you decide. I don't like my trips . I'll go wherever you want to. I do want to go someplace with you, Karl. Really. Do you believe that? I hope so. Because it's true. Take me away. Take me away, please. I can't live like other women—I'd kill myself first.

Then she opens her purse and pulls out a cigarette.

What do you think of me? she inquires in a bored voice while waiting for him to light it.

You've asked before. Quite a few times.

Tell me again. If I like what I hear you won't be sorry.

Muhlbach, holding a match, watches her cool white fingers brush deliberately against his own. The touch is as ephemeral and disturbing as that of a moth.

She seems amused. Have you had a lot of affairs since your wife died? A person with your style—do they fling themselves at you?

In a cab on the way to her apartment she abruptly rolls against him with her mouth wide open. And Muhlbach, as he strokes the lean young body and sucks her perfumed lips, admits to himself that now he is obligated. But it seems to him that he has made the right decision.

What could I have been afraid of? he asks himself while they stand side by side in the creaking elevator, clasping hands like children. Of the unknown, I guess, which is all we ever fear. I had no reason to be alarmed.

And he reflects that his ability to comprehend a slippery situation, to analyze it and make the correct decision—this ability has improved with age. Time weakens and cheats and deprives us, as everyone knows, but here and there tiny compensations spring up rather like daisies in a devastated meadow. So at least, he thinks, I have that much to be thankful for. Maybe I can't turn cartwheels the way I used to, nor do I intend to try, but quite possibly the credits equal the debits. On the whole I'm better balanced. Which means, I suppose, that I've learned to understand myself. I'm pretty sure I know where I am right now. And if I'm just a bit queasy—well, imagine how nervous I'd have been twenty years ago.

Then it occurs to him that among the many valuable things time has stolen is the capacity to feel excitement. Not totally, of course. Not yet. But take this particular situation. Years ago, he thinks, given the back seat of a taxicab or a few seconds of privacy in an elevator, how differently I'd have behaved. I'd have been steaming like a kettle. Now, although I enjoyed that little exploration in the taxi, it seems to me there's no rush. We'll be in her apartment soon enough.

He remembers Jean Gabin unbuttoning some young girl in a movie otherwise long forgotten—unbuttoning and unzipping her almost casually—and remembers the astonishment he felt that a Frenchman, especially a Frenchman, could proceed as though she were no more erotic than a soufflé. Yes. Once upon a time that had seemed very odd. But no longer. The terrible urgency of youth—Where does it go? What becomes of it?

He squints at the elevator cage, attempts to recall Gabin's features. A smashed nose, Gallic underlip, wrinkled neck. Not the face of an American screen lover. No, Gabin wasn't pretty. How old would he have been at the time? In his forties. Perhaps close to fifty.

With a screech and a bump and a jiggle the elevator stops. The doors trundle apart.

What now? he asks himself as he follows Lambeth along the musty corridor, studying the play of her hips beneath the fantastic raincoat. Am I going to regret this or not? Well, it's a bit late for second thoughts. When she rolled against me in the cab I had to decide and I did. Though actually, I think, she gave me very little choice. In any event I'm across the Rubicon. All right, so be it. But if things don't work out I won't collapse, I'll still know who I am. One of the few consolations of maturity is that we learn to accept defeat for what it is—nothing more, nothing less.

Inside the apartment Lambeth disappears, without a word of explanation, into the bedroom. Muhlbach, not certain whether to follow her or to wait, wanders around on the tatami mat with a doubtful expression, hands folded behind his back. He contemplates the apple-box bookshelves, the blowfish twisting on its string, the candle in the bottle, the dusty unwaxed floor, the prints pinned to the wall. There is a sense of impending emptiness, as though she had made up her mind to leave and in some mysterious fashion the room had been informed.

He stops at a photograph of a young naval officer in a small leatherette folder. Boyd, obviously. Handsome in a conventional way, with the straightforward innocence of so many young Americans. He couldn't have been more than twenty-five. Probably less. Well, it's a shame. He made just one mistake. Or somebody else did. Or a cable snapped or a fuse blew out, or there was a sudden gust of wind.

At that moment the telephone rings and Muhlbach feels himself stiffen. It is as if the dead boy would not let go—as if he were somewhere watching.

At last it stops. But whoever called, to judge by the length of time it kept ringing, must have known Lambeth was home.

I don't like this, he thinks with his lips compressed. I

do not like this. She attracts too many men. If I had any brains I'd get out of here. I don't know what might happen and I don't trust this girl. That Miami business would indicate she has no concept of herself, no dignity, no principles. She might be capable of anything. Of course she isn't unique. Plenty of women do what she did and it shocks me. What are they thinking? How can they give themselves to somebody they despise? I couldn't do it. I don't believe I know a man who could. There must be something fundamentally different about them. They seem to have no will of their own. They're so complaisant. I've noticed that more times than I can recall but I've never been able to get used to it. Joyce was like that. Eula. Others in the past. It astounds me. How do they justify to themselves the things they do? Yet they do, or do they? Can it be that what they do is determined by circumstances? Say the money is right, or the opportunity sounds promising, or it happens to be Wednesday, or it's begun to rain, or it's stopped raining, or Sagittarius is declining—yes, even that might be enough.

All at once he becomes aware that Lambeth has entered the room. She has exchanged the lime green chemise for a black silk nightgown and a gold necklace set with rubies.

Why are you staring? she asks, as naïve as Cinderella.

Later, feeling ineffably naked on her bed, exhausted, dizzy and stunned from such unaccustomed work, he listens to the water thundering into the bathtub and reflects on the peculiar nature of women. Lambeth, for instance, maintained that she was being killed and then unexpectedly shrieked for her mother. It would never occur to me that I was being killed, he thinks. And I certainly wouldn't call for my father. But everything evens out, I suppose. I was groaning and thrashing around like a buffalo.

He regards himself in an oval gilt mirror on the wall—studies the long flaccid unmuscled legs and arms and the hairless white torso. The body, while not too impressive, has done its job. And done it fairly well, all things considered. Not as vigorously as a quarter of a century ago perhaps, but with commendable persistence.

He attempts to see his body as Lambeth did, seeing it for the first time. This would be the body of a middle-aged gentleman, not that of a laborer. Not gone to pot, not fat, although soft. One might describe it as attenuated. The corpus of a man who has been restricted to shuffling papers, punching buttons, dictating the flow of events from a swivel chair. The result, unfortunately, is predictable. I could join a health club, he thinks. Use the pulleys and barbells. A few months with those contraptions, plus a little toasting under the sun lamp, and I'd be quite presentable. Right now—well, they say women don't pay as much attention to appearances as men do. I hope that's the case.

Lifting himself on one elbow he sucks in a deep breath and retracts his stomach. The improvement is gratifying.

He lies down, yawns, wiggles his toes.

What would it be like to have Antonio's body? To be a golden brown cat and snap your fingers for any woman you wanted. To be able to jump several feet off the ground. It's hard to imagine. It's hard to put one's self in Antonio's place, to view the world through smoldering gypsy eyes. Why is this? Why can't I empathize? he asks himself. Probably because I mistrust Spaniards and Italians and Greeks and Arabs and all the rest of those dark Mediterranean people. They look sinister. They're no more sinister than Siegfried but they do have that look about them. I don't feel at ease around them. I envy their way with women, though. I wish I didn't feel so constrained—so manacled by my Saxon heritage or by the traditions of this country. I'd love to admit my desire for women. Instead, what do I do? I pretend indifference or, at most, a sort of asexual friendliness. I'm afraid of being thought vulgar. Say I'd been on that stage, I'd never have dared save the last rose for Lambeth. Or I'd have tossed it to her in such a way as to indicate that she was simply a member of the audience. But he stalked right across to her while everybody in the theater was watching. Good God, he was about to leap off the proscenium.

Antonio, of course, belongs in Lambeth's bed—if nothing more than a physical equation is to be considered. It isn't difficult to visualize his supple flanks alongside hers, or those pale pink-tipped Northern breasts supporting the agile gypsy. Yes. Yes, they'd make a good match. But where would that leave me? In other words, if I'm not entitled to this bed whose bed would be appropriate?

True, there's Eula. There's always Eula. We fit together like ham and eggs and the union is just about as exciting. Somehow her charms don't charm me anymore. And she knows it. She keeps trying to invoke the past. 'Remember that snowy afternoon we visited the Cloisters?' 'Remember that funny little restaurant with the Australian wine?' 'Karl, do you remember . . .?' I do. I do. But it won't work. I'm sorry, Eula. Age and fat have dispelled the magnetic attraction. Nor does a cloud of lilac talcum stimulate me, in fact I have trouble breathing. Then too, your body has not only the shape but the odor of middle age, whereas Lambeth just now with the perspiration drying on her skin reminded me of—of what? Maybe a field in the country on a hot summer day.

And Eula's bedroom. Now there was a scene from the Gay Nineties. Those colored bottles on the dressing table and that old walnut Victorian furniture. Climbing into bed was like hopping in with grandmother. Of course Eula herself contributed to the effect with all those buttons and hooks and strings and snaps—it was hard to guess whether she would explode or collapse. And those underarm pads—they went out of style with bustles. And that corset. Foundation she called it. And those elastic support stockings. By the time she got rid of everything the place looked like a Goodwill store. The stockings weren't her fault, the doctor ordered those. But I couldn't face them again, probably because they remind me of my own infirmities. My eyesight. These bifocals. I used to be able to read a phone book at midnight but now the numbers might as well be chicken tracks. On the whole, though, I'm in good shape. Better than most men my age. My spine hasn't been acting up recently, which is something to be thankful for.

Anyway, I couldn't resurrect the affair with Eula. It's over. I hope I didn't hurt her feelings, it was sticky getting untangled but the situation had become intolerable. Compared to Lambeth—no, they can't be compared.

Muhlbach draws a heavy breath not only for Eula—her loneliness and her slumping attractions—but for the almost excruciating physical satisfaction he feels. Drained of desire and strength and caution, limp as a rag doll, emptier than an old tin can, he feels thoroughly at peace.

He begins to think about his wife and wonders how she might have changed if she had lived. Unlike Eula who bends the scales further each spring, Joyce probably would have lost weight, grown more subdued and introspective, because it's said we become more and more our true selves as time goes by. Joyce might have taken up weaving or découpage, immersed herself in books or medieval music, gone for solitary walks in the rain. She would not, like Eula, have listened to the siren song of the stock market or wasted hours attempting to guess which strip of concrete might quadruple in value. However it's useless to manipulate the past, nothing's served, despite what poets say.

Muhlbach, stretching luxuriously and yawning, decides that if somebody were to offer him Proust's little biscuit steeped in tea he would decline. No thanks. I'm sick of the past. Bored with the way I've been living. I don't want yesterday offered to me once again like a stale chopped liver sandwich. What I want is a change. And I deserve it. I've worked hard and I've been conscientious. As to precisely what I want, I don't know. Fresh experiences, I know that much, because somehow I'm sure I've been cheated. Too much time's been going by . . .

He pauses, arms outstretched, squinting at the ceiling, impressed by this insight.

Yes, that's true. I have been cheated. Sooner or later, of course, all of us are cheated. What chance do we have? None. Less than a trout in a barrel. One fine day when we least expect it—just when we think our problems are about to be resolved—the wave laps over us. And we never know what happened. Well, that's life, according to López. Verdad? Yes, although I don't much care for it. But at the moment the past is as irrelevant as the future. What matters to me now is now. This preposterous bird I've caught—how long can I hold her? Yes, there's the gummy problem. All I know is that I ought to keep her intrigued and satisfied as long as I can, regardless of how difficult she can be. And she is difficult. But she's worth it. I'll hang on. Within reason, of course. That is to say, I'm willing to put up with a reasonable amount of nonsense. Compromise. Sacrifice. Years ago I would have insisted on everything my own way, but that was years ago.

And as he reminds himself that very soon she will come out of the bathroom to say the tub is ready, he makes a little clucking noise. Then he continues talking to himself.

After we have our bath I suppose I ought to collect myself and go home. I shouldn't stay overnight, the children would ask where I was. And what would I tell Mrs. Grunthe? I could hardly explain, although she'd suspect. But why do I care what my housekeeper suspects? After all, she works for me, not vice versa. Lord, how many of us plod back and forth clanking with chains?

At that moment somebody taps on the door and Muhlbach sits straight up.

The tapping goes on. The water has stopped running into the tub so Lambeth must be able to hear it, however she does not come out to investigate.

I don't want any part of this, he thinks, looking around the bedroom for his clothes. I don't know what's going on but I want no part of it.

Lambeth, nude except for a peppermint-striped towel twisted around her head like a turban, saunters out of the bathroom. Obviously unconcerned, not in the least disturbed by a nocturnal visitor at her door, she lights a cigarette, seats herself on the edge of the bed and crosses her legs.

Finally the tapping stops. Footsteps can be heard going down the hall.

I wonder if I should dye my hair, she remarks. And she blows a plume of smoke and looks thoughtful.

Muhlbach, staring at her, incredulous, finds himself unable to speak or move. One of her lovers—it must have been one of her lovers—was at the door in the middle of the night and the only thing on her mind was whether or not to dye her hair. She must be pretending, but she isn't. My God, he thinks while studying her face. My God, she's serious. This is no act.

And then she goes on:

I guess I ought to tell you something. You'll hate me. I mean it's so humiliating.

She picks a shred of tobacco from her lower lip. She coughs and makes a face while he waits attentively.

Okay, I hope you're ready for it. I'm probably one of the world's worst spendthrifts.

I must have misunderstood you, he replies after thinking about this. Did you say 'spendthrift'?

She attempts to look contrite.

What in the world are you talking about? he demands. I can't understand what you're saying.

I was afraid you wouldn't, but it's real simple. I bought this dress, see, except I can't pay for it. It's a super dress. I'll wear it for you some night when we go to a far out place. But anyhow, there's this creepy old guy in the credit department who's started to bug me. He's so disgusting you just couldn't believe it. What should I do?

About the dress? he answers, unable to quit staring at her. I don't know, Lambeth. I suppose if you can't afford it you'll have to return it and hope they let you off the hook.

Are you kidding?

I don't see that you have much choice.

You bastard, she remarks with a casual air. You're like everybody else—mean and tight. You don't want to help me. You don't even like me. You got what you came for so put on your clothes and get lost.

Then she begins idly swinging one leg as though waiting for something to happen. She looks preoccupied but not anxious. Her eyes wander around the room focusing on nothing. She might be waiting for an interview. It occurs to him that perhaps her mind has slipped and she does not have the slightest idea what she has just said.

Lambeth . . . he begins, but then stops, irritated by a pleading note in his voice.

She doesn't respond. Her lips, pinched around the cigarette, expand softly while she blows another plume of smoke and goes on swinging her leg. Muhlbach, gazing at her, struggles to organize his thoughts.

I'd like to help, he continues, but I don't see how I

could. I've got two children to support and a housekeeper's salary to pay, as well as quite a few other expenses. Of course I don't know how much you owe but I get the impression it isn't a matter of fifty dollars.

Fifty dollars. Fifty dollars, she repeats with mild contempt. I shouldn't have mentioned it.

Don't talk like that. I'm glad you did. Let me consider the situation and maybe I'll come up with something.

Such as?

I know a few people. We might arrange to get that credit manager off your neck.

You're important, are you?

Stop it, Lambeth. I'm only trying to be helpful.

You're giving orders? Is that what you're all about? Is that your scene? Okay, man, just so we know where we are.

She's incoherent, he thinks. I can't follow her reasoning. She sounds disconnected. And her eyes look glassy. I wonder if she took something.

I'm going to make it big, she continues after a sudden harsh laugh. More money than I can count. It's coming down, man, it's coming down. Oh baby, is it coming down! People say that all the time, you know, like they got it made, but with me it's happening. I have this real great chart, like I told you. And there's some other stuff, too, I could tell you about. Plenty. I know what you think of me but baby you just wait.

Then to his surprise she tamps out the cigarette, stands up and saunters toward the bathroom.

In the tub she sits quietly, agreeable to suggestions, while he goes about the pleasant chore of washing her hands and arms and breasts and throat and face and then her back. And while he works he tries to imagine himself searching a chart for omens, living on expectation instead of accomplishment, squandering whatever might be in the bank because—well, because what's the point of saving money? Don't worry, the gods look after us. In regard to the mortgage, the grocer, the dentist, the pediatrician, the IRS Shylocks and everybody else—oh, never mind, something will turn up. The moon is in Pluto. Aries is rising over the Zambesi.

Yes, but all the same I should have been more sympathetic, he tells himself. She's annoyed with me, and whether she was right or I was right isn't the point. The point is that she's annoyed. That was stupid of me. I should have asked how much she owed. Maybe it's only a couple of hundred dollars. My God, I don't see how a dress could cost much more than that, not unless she commissioned it from one of those fashionable couturiers, and I don't believe she did. Anyway, I've got to face a few facts. She ignores everyday reality but I'm trying to ignore the reality of this relationship. I'd better admit that I've been lucky. For some reason she was attracted to me, but she's as unstable as a bead of mercury. The next glib young Adonis who comes along might take over my duties. Otis E. Kraft picked the wrong time or place or gambit but another one will come riding by in his Mercedes—some wavy-haired stockbroker with an inviting smile or some polo-playing attorney. Which means that if I intend to hold her I've got to raise whatever they ante. And that would be what? Modesty aside, what are my assets? All right, intelligence. I won't pretend I'm not bright. What else? A degree of aesthetic sensibility—at least I choose to think so—although that wouldn't rank too high on Lambeth's list. What next? A smattering of securities, not enough to impress her. A fairly good job providing a decent income. A reputation for integrity, and probably for sobriety. That's about the size of it. Not an overwhelming balance sheet but it just might be sufficient. She might keep me around. Longer than she kept López.

Lambeth?

What?

Lean forward.

Why?

I'll write something on your back. Try to tell me what it is.

Reluctantly, almost peevishly, she obeys.

And as she leans forward Muhlbach observes an indentation where the soft full flesh of her hips has been compressed, and it occurs to him that it is not merely the roundness that makes a female body seem precious and desirable but also, perhaps equally, these protesting little creases which are somehow comical, which appear and disappear whenever a woman moves. He stares at the subtle confluence of forms, motionless between his palms while she waits for him to began writing, and feels that he has uncovered another morsel of truth. But isn't it strange that he could have lived so long, in such close proximity to a woman, without recognizing this? He shakes his head faintly in astonishment, remembering how often he and his wife had bathed together. And on various occasions he had shared a tub with Eula—very close quarters indeed. How is it, therefore, taking into account so much experience, that a man may associate with women intimately over a period of years without learning all that can be learned?

Lambeth is impatient. What are you waiting for?

So he begins to write with his index finger on her glistening soapy skin but she deciphers the word before he can finish.

That's my name.

Very good. Now this.

Again she answers before he can finish. 'You are . . .' But what's the last word? It's too long.

'Extraordinary.'

I don't believe it.

Now once more.

After he has finished writing she sits quite still for a few seconds. Then she climbs out of the tub and begins to dry herself, keeping her face averted. Later, hugging a large pillow, she sits cross-legged on the floor watching him get dressed.

All at once she asks: Did I tell you what my father did?

Muhlbach, bending down to tie a shoelace, straightens up. What did he do?

One afternoon when I was fifteen I decided the time had come for him to teach me about love. I thought a father was supposed to make love to his daughter at a certain age. I just thought that's the way it was. I thought every father did. So I took off my clothes and went into the bedroom and said 'Here I am.' He was lying on the bed in his shorts reading the paper and he looked at me and said 'What the hell are you talking about?' So I told him what I thought he was supposed to do, and he didn't move or say anything at all for a long time but then he looked at my body again and said 'Your mother is a great lay.' So I ran into the kitchen where she was doing something—I forget what—and picked up a bread knife and tried to kill her and they took me to a psychiatrist. Do you think that was crazy? I didn't think it was. I just thought that's what fathers were supposed to do.

Well, Muhlbach answers carefully, what did the psychiatrist say?

You think I'm a nut. You do, don't you? You're just like everybody else. I'm sick of being treated like a baby. I'm sick of it! Why can't—oh never mind! Did you mean what you wrote on my back?

About loving you?

Yes. Did you mean that?

I can't be sure. I was joking, of course, because we scarcely know each other, but you've already come to mean a great deal to me.

She appears to be considering this, turning it around like a cat that has caught something unfamiliar.

Are you putting me on?

No.

Honest?

Honest.

Okay, when will I see you?

Next Saturday?

Gee, that's a long time.

I'd make it tomorrow if I could. And the night after and the night after. But we may as well be frank, Lambeth. I'm not a college kid. I could hardly make love to you like this and then get in a respectable day's work after three hours sleep. In fact I doubt if I could have done that twenty years ago.

Instead of answering she hugs the pillow. She looks at him without blinking, inexpressively.

Well, he thinks while buttoning his shirt, she's gone again. For a minute there I had the feeling we were actually communicating but now I don't know where she is, maybe on the other side of the moon.

He picks up his necktie and turns to the mirror. Lambeth, tell me . . .

But she shakes her head. No questions.

All right. As you wish.

Alone in the elevator he has no trouble finishing the question: Tell me, Lambeth, who was at the door?

The mysterious night visitor may live in the building so Muhlbach peers through the metal grill of the elevator before stepping into the lobby. But it is also possible that he may be hanging around outside, so an examination of the street seems prudent. However the street looks no more menacing than usual.

I doubt if it could have been López, he says to himself while waiting for a cab. I get the feeling López is done for. If they'd had a fight it would be a different story. In that case they might reconcile and I'd find myself squeezed out. When a woman becomes bored, though, that's the end. Well, I see why she was bored. López can be clever, even brilliant in a superficial way with his anecdotes and compliments. But he does get tiresome.

THREE days later, preoccupied with thoughts of a forthcoming business conference, waiting to cross at 53rd and Lexington, Muhlbach observes a dejected rumpled Latin slowly emerge from the subway. At that instant the light changes.

Across the intersection, having once again beaten the odds, he turns around. But López, if indeed it was López, has disappeared. That's who it must have been, he thinks. But the man looked like a derelict, more dead than alive. He needed a shave and he must have been sleeping in that suit. I wonder what's happened. Lambeth couldn't be responsible. He was unhappy about losing her, of course, but this fellow looked suicidal. Maybe I should try to find him.

For a few moments he considers the idea. However nobody in such a condition would want to be accosted.

Well! he reflects, walking up Lexington. I must say that was a sight. López doesn't mean anything to me, just the same I hate to see a man fall apart. It's curious, too, because at La Galette he seemed all right. Nervous, certainly. Yes, he was extremely nervous—tearing the bread to bits—and his hands trembled. But at least he managed to control himself, whereas this fellow appeared to have given up. What a shame. I might ask Lambeth about him next Saturday.

Saturday, according to Lambeth, would be impossible. An old friend, somebody she hasn't seen in ages, will be arriving.

Muhlbach suggests Friday.

That won't do either. Maybe next week, she adds. Sweetheart, I want to. Honest. Only this weekend would be kind of awkward.

Muhlbach attempts to give the impression that he too might find the following week more convenient.

Oh hey! she cries. Guess what! I started your collage.

My collage?

Did you forget?

Certainly not. I'm looking forward to it. When may I see it?

When I get it finished.

Tell me, what colors are you using?

I won't tell you because it's supposed to be a surprise, but you're going to love it. Anyway I sure hope you do.

I know I will. I'm anxious to see it. And I miss you.

No kidding?

More than I thought I would.

I miss you, too. Bye!

That was fast, he reflects while rocking around in the swivel chair. It's almost as though she didn't want to talk to me. I wonder if I could have said something offensive the other night. No, I must be imagining. She feels obligated to entertain her friend, which is understandable. But I did want to see her, more than I like to admit. As a matter of fact I'm getting attached to her, which is foolish. She's bad news, as Otto would say. And I can guess what Mrs. Grunthe would say about her. Perhaps it's just as well she's busy this weekend, I'll have a chance to analyze the situation. I do like her—one moment I do—but then I don't. And who's this 'old friend'? Some girl, presumably, though she wasn't specific, so it might be a man. But that's unimportant. Unless, of course, she plans to spend the weekend with an ex-lover, and I suspect there may be more than a few of those. In fact the eastern seaboard is probably crawling with them. But this is absurd, I can't waste time drumming up imaginary infidelities.

Frowning, very much dissatisfied, Muhlbach hooks on his glasses and returns to work.

But a sheaf of statistics pertaining to Metropolitan's

tentative merger with Occidental Life and Casualty cannot jog the mind or senses as sweetly as the recollection of Lambeth's soapy sinuous body between his knees in the fragrant bathtub. He remembers, too, how she had lain underneath him with her lips slightly parted, her cheeks suffused with color.

All at once he wakes up, blinking, and slaps the desk in exasperation.

Later it occurs to him that she might have been forced to break the date not because she preferred to be with somebody else but because she had no choice. And the longer he contemplates this possibility the more reasonable it sounds. He reminds himself that he does not know much about her. Very little indeed. She does a certain amount of modeling. Her fiancé died in a crash at Pensacola. What else? Apparently her father was in the garment business, which could explain how she met Izzy. And she is reputed to be a heavy drinker, according to Eula. But I haven't noticed that, he thinks. She wasn't drinking at La Galette, except for wine, nor with me the night we went to see Antonio. All right, what else? At the party there was quite a lot of gossip but nothing significant. Double entendres, mostly. Allusions to her morals. Pure gossip. Malicious compliments. The fact is I know nothing about the girl. I don't know any of her friends. I haven't the slightest idea what sort of people she associates with, which may be no loss because I doubt if I'd care for them. And isn't it peculiar that she came to the party alone! Of course she might have arranged to meet somebody there, but except for López and Baxter the only one I recall was Veach—and he was lying. I've never heard such a transparent lie. She couldn't possibly have been attracted to him. Nor would she have gone for that ass Baxter. And López had never seen her until that night. But whether or not she had a date isn't important, what I'd like to know is who she could have met at the party. There were several bright young executives but they look so much alike these days—muttonchop Edwardian caricatures. Checker-board trousers and curled hair. I can't quite see Lambeth waltzing away with one of those. A dark sleek Cosa Nostra type, maybe. So let's assume she did meet one, which is not impossible. If some hoodlum put her to work modeling stolen jewelry—yes, that could explain her 'awkward' weekend. I must say she didn't sound quite like herself on the phone, as though somebody might have been in the apartment. I wonder. No. No, I'm concocting scenarios. Stolen jewelry and Sicilians with diamond cufflinks. I must be losing my mind. I ought to accept the situation gracefully, much as I'd like to see her. I'd totally forgotten her existence until last week and now I act as though one more week without her would be unbearable. I'll see her soon enough, Saturday after this. In the meantime I could send a few flowers. A dozen roses. I could sign the card 'Antonio.' She'd know who sent them. On the other hand that might not be appropriate, she doesn't have much sense of humor. Anyway, flowers would be a good idea.

So, Monday morning en route to work he visits the florist.

By noon the roses should have been delivered, but there is no response from Lambeth.

Nor has she called by five o'clock.

At home that night, questioning Mrs. Grunthe, he

learns that there have been only two telephone calls. One was a gentleman offering a six-week course in ballroom dancing at a special discount. The other wanted to come by and demonstrate a vacuum cleaner.

Now come to think of it, Mrs. Grunthe goes on while drying the soup tureen. Come to think of it now, there was a lady called. Ah, I didn't like the sound of her. A bad one, if you ask me.

Oh? And what did she want? Muhlbach asks as casually as possible.

After an interminable length of time Mrs. Grunthe ends the suspense:

Taking a nationwide poll of the brand of cereal we buy. Shredded cardboard is what I told her—all of it. Filthy filthy stuff. Bad for the teeth of children. A crime, I told her. A crime. You should be in jail, that's what I said. Ah, she didn't care for that, she didn't. Not a whit. You should have heard the splutter. I doubt she'll trouble us again, not while I'm here. A shame, the use they put to the telephone. And I was in the middle of laundry. Jail's too good for them, it is.

Nobody else?

Not a soul. Them three. Three too many.

Miss Brent may call tomorrow. If she does, Mrs. Grunthe, please don't give her an argument. Just take the message.

I am not given to argument, sir. I'm looking out for your best interest, you and the children, which is my understanding I was employed to do. Now if you find me unsatisfactory . . .

Of course not. Absolutely not, Mrs. Grunthe, you're doing a wonderful job. But just in case Miss Brent should happen to telephone, you'll be sure to take the message?

Without fail, sir. Without fail.

There is no response from Lambeth on Tuesday—not at the office, not at home—and he begins to wonder if the flowers were delivered. Possibly there was a mix-up. It isn't likely, but on the other hand common courtesy would dictate an acknowledgment. However I won't call, he tells himself. It's up to her. She should make the next move. I don't understand why she doesn't have the decency to let me know she received them.

By five o'clock Wednesday his resolve has crumbled:

Lambeth? Sorry to disturb you but I was curious. I ordered some roses a few days ago . . .

She answers in a cold sullen voice that the roses were delivered. Then she adds that she does not like presents.

What? he asks after a moment. What did you say?

I said I hate being given things. I hate it!

Is this some kind of a joke? The other night you were annoyed with me because I wouldn't help you out on that dress.

Oh, leave me alone, she replies. I never asked you to call. Leave me alone why don't you.

Lambeth, please, don't be rude. I thought you'd like the flowers. I had no idea you'd be irritated. I wouldn't have sent them if I'd known. Most women enjoy little gifts.

Little gifts. Little gifts, she repeats contemptuously.

Oh. I see. So that's how it is.

That's how it is. Are you shocked?

More than anything else I'm puzzled.

I really get sick of people saying that. 'Lambeth, I don't understand you.' 'Lambeth, I can't figure you out.' Okay, don't try.

I'd like to know more about you.

Forget it.

I must admit you're not easy.

Did I tell you I was?

No.

Did you think I was? Do I look easy?

No.

Hey, wait a minute—somebody's at the door.

Muhlbach shuts his eyes. I can't take this, he thinks. I feel like an idiot. I ought to hang up.

Lambeth returns sooner than expected. Listen, Karl, I'm sorry but I'm kind of busy. Maybe we can talk some other time.

All right. But as long as I've got you on the phone let's decide about Saturday.

Saturday?

We do have a date, don't we?

Actually, I have this job either Friday or Saturday night, only I won't know which until the last second.

What sort of job?

It's a modeling assignment. Actually it's not really definite. I mean I might be out of town for a while, like three or four days.

In other words you don't care to see me.

I promised I'd do this job. I didn't know when I was going to hear from you. You can't expect me to sit around waiting, can you?

You aren't making sense, Lambeth. The last time we talked we agreed on this Saturday.

Well, I forgot.

What's wrong? Please tell me.

Nothing.

There is.

Stop bugging me, Karl.

All right, I'm sorry. No further questions.

Okay. Wow, you sure are uptight. Listen, I've got to run.

Lambeth, just one minute. Do you remember when we were joking about taking a trip? We were having supper after the show and we joked about the Riviéra and so forth. Do you remember?

Uh huh. That was fun.

Yes, it was. Well, I've got an idea. Why don't we rent a car and get out of the city for a few days? We could go for a drive through Connecticut. How does that sound? Have you ever been to Essex?

No.

It's a lovely, quiet town. We could stay at the Griswold, which is delightful, and we could have a picnic beside the river. Or there's a marvelous old Colonial place in Ridgefield called Stonehenge. Joyce and I stayed there years ago. There were counterpanes on the bed and a fireplace in the room and a bottle of iced wine in a bucket waiting for us when we arrived. It was wonderful, so private and relaxing. Or if you wouldn't mind a longer drive we could try the Red Lion in Stockbridge, up in the Berkshires, which is a bit more modern—a big white hotel with a posh dining room and a very good menu. Large bedrooms. Nice views. What do you say?

I don't know. I'll think about it.

Oh, wait! Don't hang up. I remembered another—an old manor house above Norfolk, close to Marlboro. I haven't stayed at this place but I understand it's highly recommended—New England atmosphere and so forth. I could find out more and let you know.

Okay.

Shall I make a reservation?

No, just find out more about it. I'm sort of busy right now. These guys are here.

I could arrange to leave the office early Friday afternoon, which would give us the entire weekend.

Not this weekend.

I'm not pressing you. Tentatively suppose we plan on the weekend after this. I realize you're in a hurry. I'll talk to you again soon.

Okay. Bye.

After the call Muhlbach sits at his desk for a long time with his head in his hands. Suddenly he jumps up and begins walking rapidly back and forth. What am I doing? he asks aloud. I don't know what's gotten into me. I have no business chasing around with a girl that age. It's humiliating. Besides, she's neurotic and dangerous. I've got to break this off. All right, I will. When I talk to her I'll say I've changed my mind—I'm sorry but we've got to end it.

And as soon as he has made this decision it seems not only correct but inevitable. Yes, he thinks, I was deluding myself. She couldn't care about a man so much older. She lacks the sensitivity. Of course that's not entirely her fault, she's young and most young girls are the same way. 'Is he good-looking?' That's what they want to know. Never 'Is he intelligent?' Or 'Is he decent and thoughtful and courteous?' And naturally they want to know how much money he'll spend. Well, it's too bad. What a shame. Yes, what a shame! he thinks, standing at the window with his arms crossed, gazing down on the traffic. I wish we'd been able to get to know each other. We could have gone places and done things together. And I suppose it's remotely possible that we might have fallen in love. But all she wants from life is to make it big—whatever that means. Money, obviously. A prestigious address. Charge accounts. Hobnobbing with celebrities in Puerto Vallarta, et cetera, et cetera. But at least I found out in time, I have that much to be thankful for. I'd have destroyed myself financially as well as emotionally.

He walks away from the window with a bemused expression, pinching the tip of his nose and asking himself how he could have failed to recognize anything so obvious. How strange that in spite of seeing what happened to López he himself had very nearly dropped into the same pit. Well, I certainly wasn't paying attention, he reflects, because God knows the evidence came stumbling out of the subway. And that evening at La Galette he tried to warn me. But I only nodded and pretended to listen. Apparently I was hypnotized by Lambeth. Whatever he said went through my head like the first day of spring. Well, now I know. And just in time. All right, the matter's settled. Our unlikely affair has just come skidding to a stop.

The following afternoon while engrossed in a new actuarial report he is interrupted by Gloria. Miss Brent is calling.

No, tell her I'm busy. Wait. Let me have it.

I might as well get this over with, he thinks, picking up the telephone. I'd rather not talk to her but there's no sense putting it off.

Hi! she begins. Have you got a sec?

Why, hello Lambeth, he answers. The fact is I'm pretty busy, but of course I have a few seconds. What's on your mind?

You must be furious.

Furious?

I acted like a bitch. Didn't you hate me?

I was disappointed, I wouldn't deny that. But no doubt you had your reasons. And then, appalled by the sound, Muhlbach hears himself chuckle.

You mean you're not sore?

Certainly not.

I was kind of embarrassed.

Nonsense, Lambeth. There's no reason for you to feel that way.

Well anyhow, thanks for being so nice. Hey listen, you invited me to go for a drive.

Yes. So I did, he answers, suddenly pressing the telephone against his ear.

Do you still want me?

Oh Lambeth! What a question!

Okay, let's do it. I really feel like splitting. And I don't mean next Friday—I mean now.

Today?

Right now. How soon can you pick me up?

But we can't go today. I've got a job. I can't simply put on my hat and waltz out of the office. I'd love to, believe me, but there's a conference this afternoon and I've got several appointments.

While he waits for her to answer it occurs to him that he has remained absolutely motionless since she mentioned the trip. I must look like somebody in a wax museum, he thinks, leaning back in the chair but keeping the phone pressed tightly against his ear.

After a long silence Lambeth starts to complain. Friday is so far off. She wants to go now. And Muhlbach, listening tensely, believes he can hear a note of resignation underneath the complaint.

Friday is much too far off, he agrees. I'm as anxious to get away as you are, but it's just not possible. Now where shall we go? Did any of the places I mentioned sound appealing? Because I should make a reservation. Unless, of course, we just elect to follow the open road.

Lambeth doesn't care. As long as they get out of the city, nothing else matters.

What's wrong?

Don't ask dumb questions.

Sorry.

What do you want me to wear?

Let's be comfortable. Slacks or jeans—whatever you like. And in regard to our destination, suppose we sail with the wind. Let's plan on two nights, possibly three. It will depend on my schedule. I hope we can have three nights.

I ought to get back Sunday. I have this appointment Sunday night. And don't ask me what it's about.

That was the last thing on my mind.

Okay, great. What time?

I'll pick you up at three-thirty.

Don't be late. Bye.

I can't understand this, he thinks, rubbing his hands briskly. I'm not even sure how I feel. It's exciting, of course, although she certainly poisoned the water with that remark about a Sunday appointment.

During the next few days he often finds himself staring at a memo he has just finished reading, or at a letter he has dictated and is expected to sign, and discovers that he does not know what it says. Nor can he forget the 'appointment.' The word has an ugly overtone. If she had simply made a date for Sunday evening why wouldn't she say so? Why refer to it as an appointment? And he torments himself with other questions that cannot be answered: Does she really intend to go? What if she isn't there when I go by to pick her up? Why did she suddenly change her mind? Who else has she been seeing? Or suppose she changes her mind again—because she's capable of that. Well, I've either struck gold or put my foot in something. I'm not sure I want to find out which, but there's no turning back.

On Friday, just when he is about to leave the office, Gloria announces that Miss Cunningham is on the phone.

I told her you were in a rush to get away, Gloria adds around the chewing gum, but she insisted it was an emergency. If you ask me she's a kook.

I appreciate your opinion, Muhlbach answers. Now will you put her through? Ah! Hello, Eula. What's the emergency?

After the usual preliminaries what it comes down to is that he has neglected to call. You dreadful man, she continues, I haven't heard from you in ages. I've been worred sick. How on earth are you?

I'm fine, he replies more brusquely than he had intended. I've been rather tied up, Eula. Was there something specific you wanted to talk about? Because I'm just on the point of leaving.

Oh, I should say there is! I found the nicest turkey in the freezer and I want you to come for dinner tonight. Now don't you dare refuse because I won't hear of it.

Tonight would be impossible. Thanks for the invitation but I'll be out of the city all weekend.

Where are you going?—if I may be so bold.

I'm not sure.

I beg your pardon? You're 'not sure.' Is that what you said?

That's correct. I've rented a car and I intend to go for a drive through the countryside.

Eula's shrill laughter flutters along the wire. You're not inviting me?

I've already made plans.

You beast!

Muhlbach glances at his watch. Thank you again, Eula. Sorry I won't be able to make it. Now I've got to be going.

What sort of car did you rent?

One of those Japanese bugs.

Aren't they risky?

I have no reason to think so.

Won't you have a problem with those long legs?

I'll manage.

Is it blue?

Muhlbach takes a deep breath. I have no idea what color it is, Eula. Furthermore, as long as it runs I don't give a damn.

You're such a grouch.

I apologize if I sound rude but I was halfway to the door when you called.

Then for goodness sake don't let me delay you. I wouldn't dream of interfering with your drive through the countryside—not for all the tea in China. Will you be taking a little companion?

Eula, we have known each other for several years. Would you do me a favor?

I might. What?

As my son would say: Cool it.

My word, Karl, if that's how you feel. I simply thought you'd enjoy a turkey dinner.

Some other evening.

Is that a promise? Cross your heart?

Yes. Now good-bye.

Do you like beef Stroganoff?

You are trying to detain me. Good-bye.

I'm jealous. Who is she?

My little companion? Her name is YoKo Kimono. She's an excellent mechanic.

After a moment Eula replies briskly: I do hope it rains. I hope it utterly pours.

Then she hangs up.

On the way to Lambeth's apartment Muhlbach defends himself. Eula herself is to blame, she was the one who called. It's too bad she is lonely or jealous or whatever, but who's at fault? She is. What could be more obvious? It's as plain as the eye of a blackbird. Instead of minding her own business she got nosy. Maybe I should have told the truth, that might have turned her off once and for all. Now I'm committed to another evening with her. I should have said Lambeth Brent, Eula. You remember Lambeth—that succulent little blonde at the party whose throat you wanted to slit. That's who my companion will be. And as for rain—sorry old girl, not a cloud in the sky.

But why did she choose that precise instant to call? Incredible. Women seem to have evolved a special sense which alerts them to imminent happenings—some sort of vestigial survival apparatus, no doubt because they've been obliged to deal with men for so many generations. But how does it operate?

Stopped momentarily in traffic not far from a delicatessen Muhlbach is reminded of his promise to have dinner with Eula. Then he begins to think about the last meal she cooked. She was so proud of it, and the food was atrocious. The salad wasn't bad but the asparagus had a peculiar medicinal flavor. So did the coffee—a very odd taste. And the chicken. Ah yes, the chicken. That chicken was so raw it squeaked. As a matter of fact Lambeth probably could have cooked a better meal. Yet why do I assume Lambeth is a poor cook? She might not be bad. Adequate, at least. But for some reason it's hard to visualize her among the pots and pans. I always think of her lying next to me with that platinum hair spread across the pillow like a shampoo ad. Or else I see her doubled up like a picture in one of those Oriental sex manuals.

Somebody's secretary, almost certainly a secretary, has paused on the sidewalk to appraise her reflection in the delicatessen window. It occurs to Muhlbach that Lambeth would never do that. Lambeth is vain, of course. Impossibly vain. But glancing at herself in a shop window is hardly necessary. She knows what she looks like. She can see herself reflected in the faces of people staring at her. The last thing she needs is reassurance. And yet she does. Once in a while it shows. She gets as jumpy as a grasshopper. What's the explanation?

The light changes, he shifts into gear, turns west on 72nd street, and resumes talking to himself.

Maybe the explanation is that she's not terribly bright. An average mind, more or less average, warped out of shape by too much attention. Getting upset when I mentioned those crystal gimcracks—as though I'd accused her of stealing them! What a stupid response. No, not 'stupid' so much as unreasonable. Because she is unreasonable. Obstinate. Selfish. Although I've got to make some allowance for her sex. It could be all that reproductive paraphernalia. Eula runs amuck once in a while, going through one or another of her moon phases. Joyce did too, which always astonished me, she was so controlled. But neither of them ever behaved as outrageously as Lambeth. It might be smart to keep my eyes open. I'd as soon not end this trip with a pair of scissors in my back.

Then, recalling the conversation with Eula, he wags his head. It's too bad, but when a house reaches a certain age there's no use attempting to renovate. A fresh coat of paint won't help. You just move out. We could be friends, go to parties and so forth, but as for sharing a bed—no. Kaput. Terminado. I've lost the urge. She's too matronly. She reminds me of those stout women at rummage sales and PTA meetings. And in bed she flounders around like a beached porpoise. What does Lambeth remind me of? Well, she could be likened to a young fox or a trapped bird—any number of things, I suppose, but comparisons are a little silly. That lime-green number she wore to the performance, though—I did feel as if I were with a chorus girl. Let's hope she picked something conservative for the trip.

LAMBETH has her own idea about an appropriate traveling ensemble: a lavender suit with flared trousers fitted to her rump like sausage casing. It may reveal a trifle less and be not quite so fluorescent as the colored handkerchief that won Antonio's heart, but in a Connecticut village it should bring everybody to the window. As for checking in at a motel—I'll have to park out of sight, he thinks. I can just see myself writing 'Mr. and Mrs. Karl Muhlbach' with me dressed as I am and Lambeth right outside the manager's office in that Japanese kamikaze. Oh yes, yes, we've been married a long time, Mrs. Peabody. We have thirteen children, would you believe it? You wouldn't? Neither would I. Well, to a certain extent this is my own fault. I should have gone shopping, bought something sporty—a plaid coat or a turtleneck and some sunglasses. Maybe a cap. The way I'm dressed anybody would think I was going to a board meeting.

Ah ha! So! he exclaims, clapping his hands. All set, Lambeth?

Lambeth does not sound enthusiastic. She mentions again that she must get back Sunday, by noon if possible.

Muhlbach essays a little joke: he suggests that after a couple of days she might never want to come back. The joke does not succeed. A look of contempt or of terrible cynicism passes across her face.

Nor does she approve of the car. Maybe she was expecting a Mercedes. Once inside, however, she becomes less querulous. The bucket seat is comfortable and there's plenty of leg room. She asks how fast it will go.

Muhlbach, uncertain, peers at the speedometer. The dial goes up to one hundred and twenty.

I've only been driving it a few minutes, he answers, so I can't say, but it zips right along. I had no trouble at all beating a yellow light on Broadway. And another thing, he continues, slumping behind the wheel in order to avoid hitting his head on the roof, these seats recline. You'll find a handle there on the side next to the floor.

Almost at that instant Lambeth drops out of sight.

Shit, she mutters, pulling herself up. I think I hurt my neck. Why didn't you warn me?

I was about to. Are you all right?

It isn't serious, I guess. Let's get started. If we're going we might as well go.

Muhlbach guns the engine, taps the horn—which does not sound particularly authoritative—and darts jerkily into traffic.

Halfway through the Bronx the gearshift begins to stick. A certain amount of jiggling solves the problem, temporarily at least. But now a sinister ragged black-bellied cloud trailing poisonous green tendrils has drifted out of the north. The signs are not auspicious.

Lambeth, her features as threatening as the cloud, snaps on the radio and begins punching buttons. She locates a rock station. Muhlbach decides not to object. If she has found something to enjoy, anything, even this simpleminded screaming—well, that's what counts.

Wah-wah! says the radio. Wah-wah-wah! Baby! Baby! Rockababy! Rockababy! All night! All night long! Wah-wah-wah! And so on.

In a few minutes Lambeth is bored. Off goes the radio. Out comes another cigarette. She smokes moodily, looking straight ahead, every ten seconds flicking ashes at the window. Evidently she does not intend to open her mouth until Sunday. But all at once she asks about the children. Were they upset when they learned he was going away?

Donna was. Otto didn't care. In fact he was probably relieved. He's learned how to manipulate the housekeeper, which means the TV will be on twenty-four hours a day.

Lambeth considers this information. Do they miss their mother? she asks in a hostile voice.

I suppose they do. They must. But they don't talk about her anymore, which surprises me.

What do they talk about?

School. What happened at school. What happened on the playground. Somebody hit somebody or somebody pulled somebody's hair. That kind of thing. I suppose it's what all of us talked about at that age.

Uh huh, she answers. I guess.

Do you want children, Lambeth?

Like I want leprosy.

You might change your mind in a year or so.

Nope.

They can break your heart a thousand ways, but there are compensations.

That's not my scene. I couldn't handle the housewife bit.

Never?

I'd go to prison first.

Why do you say that?

I'm tired of being used. Man, you don't know how I've been used. But I'm not going to tell you, so don't ask. The scum I've met—oh Jesus!

In that case why do you keep on modeling? Why not give it up? Try something else.

Such as? Be a manicurist? Sell Avon cosmetics? I

mean, you're kidding! Could you see me doing that? She laughs bitterly. Like if I could just get a break—one real decent break.

Ah yes, Muhlbach says to himself while she goes on talking. If. If. How familiar that sounds. If somebody would give me a break. Why won't anybody help me? Won't somebody please give me a chance?

Finally he interrupts: Nobody's going to give you a break, Lambeth. You may as well get used to the idea. Your career means absolutely nothing to anybody except yourself.

That's not true.

It is true.

You sound so damn sure.

That's right, I am. Nothing marvelous and unexpected is about to happen. The telegram saying you won the sweepstakes will never arrive. And the reason it won't is because I've never gotten it and I don't know anybody else who has.

That doesn't prove anything.

Suit yourself.

Well, I don't want to believe it.

I don't want to believe it either.

But you do? You really do? Listen, if you believe that how can you go on living? I mean, what is there to look forward to?

Quite a bit. Nothing dramatic, perhaps. Nothing exhilarating. But quite a bit.

I don't see life that way. I want too much. I'll never settle for a Mickey Mouse apartment with a nice-guy husband. No way. I'd freak.

You misunderstand. I want more. Of course I want more. I didn't say I was satisfied. I'd love to be rich. I'd like nothing better than to be able to afford that Mediterranean excursion. Drop in on the Prince and so forth. Do you think I enjoy being crammed into a bus every morning? Don't be ridiculous! I'm far from satisfied with my life. Well, no, that's not strictly accurate, because things could be worse. The insurance business isn't bad, it's all right. I'm grateful I'm not locked into a job I despise. But if you think just because I don't live extravagantly—just because I visit the barber every so often—and read the financial page—and try to set aside enough so my children can go to college—if you—well, never mind! Never mind. I'm sorry. I don't know what got into me.

Hey, she murmurs. Cool it, huh? You just about flipped.

All I meant to say, Lambeth, was that I've been toting the barge and lifting the bale or whatever it is long enough to realize that my life will never change. I'll do what I do as long as I live. I'll never touch the rainbow. And I don't think you will either. I'd love to, and I hope you do. I doubt if we will. This isn't good news, I admit. I'd rearrange the situation if I could, nearer to the heart's desire. In fact, as somebody said, though I can't remember who: 'Life being what it is, one dreams of revenge.'

Do you believe in love? she asks, looking at him narrowly.

Of course.

Could you love somebody like me? I mean me personally. The other night you said you could.

You sound desperate. Do you need so much to be loved?

I'm terrified.

What frightens you?

Tomorrow. Tomorrow and tomorrow and tomorrow. I don't know what's going to happen. I've had it with two-room apartments. Oh man, I'm sick of asking the fucking super to turn up the heat and put a new lock on my door and all the rest of that shit.

Now what's the point of such language? he wonders, tightening his grip on the wheel. What does it accomplish? All she does is cheapen herself. Maybe she's trying to shock me, it sounded that way. But why?

Lambeth, just as though she could read his mind, suddenly touches off a string of obscenities and waits to see what effect this will have.

None of the expressions are original. They are not even imaginatively joined. Muhlbach decides there would be no sense in acknowledging them. The naïve attempt at vulgarity is tiresome and any kind of response would probably encourage her to try again.

What a drag, she mutters. I could kick myself.

A few minutes later she shakes her head in exasperation. Forty miles an hour! We'll never get anyplace. It bugs me going this slow. I mean it doesn't make any sense.

Do you have an appointment?

Oh, drop dead. I think I'll take a nap.

She yanks the handle, stretches out on the seat and shuts her eyes. Motionless, rigid with scorn and displeasure, arms folded across her breast, she resembles an effigy on the lid of a sarcophagus.

It occurs to him that perhaps he should have gone traveling with Eula. It might be like traveling with Brunhilde but at least the amenities would be preserved. None of these preposterous eruptions. Conversation would be easier, more civilized. It might not be exciting but it certainly would be more comfortable. Yes, he thinks, tapping his fingers on the steering wheel, after all, Eula and I speak the same language. And that does make things easier. I could say, for example, that I liked such and such a Tommy Dorsey tune without being obliged to explain who Dorsey was. Also, people on the road wouldn't gawk at us, they'd take it for granted that we were husband and wife. I must admit I don't like being stared at. Yes, it might have been smarter to bring Eula. If only I could feel something for her. She must have been reasonably seductive when she was Lambeth's age. Well, more than 'reasonably.' She still has a nice complexion. She must have been as plump and rosy as one of Renoir's big healthy girls. Now, of course, she's fighting gravity. Too many hills and dales. What a shame. If only I were an Arab I could have invited them both. Although that might be no bed of roses either.

Around a bend in the road he swerves to avoid a scruffy little dog. Lambeth opens her eyes and sits up.

How was the nap?

I wasn't asleep, I was thinking. Where are we?

The compass is broken but I believe we're off the coast of Sumatra. What were you thinking about?

Us.

Your disposition has improved. You sound almost cheerful.

I needed a vacation. My nerves were shot. I got a feeling I could be getting an ulcer.

Not at your age.

You can be so damn positive! But I like you anyhow, she adds, touching his knee. Where do you want to stop tonight?

That may depend on the gearshift.

Why didn't you rent a better car? Hey look, I didn't mean that. I'm sorry. I'm always in a bad mood this time of the month. Then, after a pause, she continues: You don't need to give me the fish eye. Do you think I planned this? Oh shit, you do! 'That dirty bitch!'—that's what you're saying to yourself.

Lambeth, please.

Now you're really uptight. You are, aren't you? Well, I didn't plan this. I don't like it any more than you do. It's just that I'm irregular. Honest. Listen, Karl, I'll make it up to you.

Suppose we change the subject.

Do you believe me?

Yes. All right.

Cross your heart? Hope to die? Come on, say it!

You're impossible.

Okay, what else is new?

Tell me about that credit manager. Is he still causing trouble?

He's no problem. I could get rid of him in five minutes.

How?

Don't be stupid.

This was a mistake, Muhlbach thinks. We won't last two days. I guess I'm a romantic, expecting a beautiful woman to act like a lady. She is what she is and there's nothing I can do about it. But I don't like it.

Paying for the dress doesn't seem to worry you anymore. Has something else come up?

Lambeth takes a nail file out of her purse before answering. Yeah, well, this guy I used to live with—he wants us to get married.

You sound as if you don't much care for him.

I do, sort of. Only he gets these weird ideas. You wouldn't believe half of what I could tell you. He's a podiatrist—a foot doctor. Actually he's not a doctor yet. He's what they call a 'resident.' Anyway, he wants to open his own clinic next year in Jefferson City. He and this older guy about your age are going into partnership.

Jefferson City? Missouri?

Uh huh. That's where he's from. He says they could make a lot of bread if they bought their own building. I never heard of doctors doing that, did you?

It isn't unusual. So you'd be moving to the Midwest. That would be quite a change.

Really! Do you know any podiatrists?

Why do you ask?

I was curious how much they make.

You seem less interested in the man than in what he could provide.

He's a groovy guy, Lambeth remarks while inspecting her nails. We dig each other.

Let me tell you something, my wild young swan, marrying somebody is serious business. When I asked Joyce to marry me I doubt if she gave a thought to how much I was earning, or would ever earn. And if she did I'm sure it was a secondary consideration.

Don't get mad.

Did you hear a word I said?

Not really. I like you, Karl. You're a nice man and I don't meet too many nice men. But you sure can be a drag. Listen, she continues a moment later while frowning at her nails, you'll think this is a put-on but I've thought a lot about us. I mean a lot.

I'd like to believe that.

Only you don't because of how I treat you. Is that the message?

Perhaps.

Well, you just don't appreciate my situation. There are all kinds of things about me you don't know. I mean I'd explain if I could, but it would be dangerous. Like—nope, I'm not going to say a word. All I'm going to tell you is this: they tried to kill me.

Who did?

That's all I can tell you.

'They.' The mysterious omnipresent and extremely convenient enemies who make life difficult. Well, he thinks, I won't buy it. I don't know what she's been up to but I can't imagine anybody attempting to kill her. Not that they wouldn't feel like it. But as for an actual attempt, no. She's lying. No, not lying—just fabricating. Dramatizing. Day to day life isn't enough for her, she's got to pretend. Visit the Burtons in Mexico. Hide-and-seek with killers. She's a child. I wonder if she was always like this or if the death of that Navy pilot may have affected her mind.

When her fiancé is mentioned Lambeth shrugs. She remarks that she has practically forgotten him.

Is that true?

Okay, I keep his picture.

I daresay he meant more to you than this podiatrist.

Sure. But me and Boyd could never have made it.

Why not?

He came from this real rich Philadelphia family. He went to Princeton and he had class, you know. When I met his old man I felt like the scavenger's daughter.

Why do you denigrate yourself?

What does that mean?

To run yourself down. Why do it? You must know the effect you create. People stop talking when you go by. Even the children pause.

Listen, Karl, I'm so tired of being stared at I could puke. Sometimes I get asked for my autograph because people think I'm a movie star. You know what I want to do? I want to write in great huge letters 'Nobody!'

Say you were plain, would you be happier?

I want to be noticed for myself, not because—oh hey! Look! Over there in the field! Look at the bull!

Muhlbach lifts his foot from the accelerator.

That would be a cow, I think.

It's got horns. Are you sure it isn't a bull? It's so big. Oh, yeah, you're right. Hey, what brand is it?

Breed, not brand. It's a Holstein.

How can you tell?

By the color.

Far out. Gee, that's the first cow I've seen in years. It's great being in the country. I really enjoy this.

Me too. Now what were we talking about?

I forget.

So do I. But it doesn't matter.

No, it certainly doesn't, he repeats to himself. What's important is that maybe this trip wasn't such a mistake. Maybe we'll find out what we have in common. Maybe we'll make it. I hope so. This could be a beginning. And it seems to him just as the car passes over the crest of a delightful little hill sprinkled with wild flowers that almost anything is possible.

I better tell you this before I lose my nerve, Lambeth remarks, looking for something in her purse. Only you've got to promise you won't turn around and start back to New York.

Muhlbach smiles. We won't be turning around. A while ago I was afraid we might, but not now. What do you want to tell me?

Well, she answers after lighting a cigarette, here goes. I got in some trouble.

Inevitably.

Listen. Be serious. I almost went to prison.

Because you were a public menace?

Karl, please. Don't you want to hear?

Yes. I'm listening.

It was no joke. I got busted for stealing.

What did you steal?

A bottle of perfume.

Why?

Because. I've boosted stuff ever since I can remember.

So Veach was right, he thinks. Well, I don't care. I stole a couple of magazines when I was a kid. Some other stuff, too. Candy bars and so forth. It's part of growing up, proving how smart you are.

He looks at her, but her face reveals nothing. She aims a plume of smoke at the windshield.

Most of the time I steal clothes. Fur coats especially. You think I'm kidding, only I'm not.

How many fur coats have you stolen?

Eight.

How do you do it? I can see making off with a bottle of perfume or some lipstick, but you couldn't tuck a fur coat under your blouse.

Aren't you horrified?

That you're a thief? Don't be silly. Now tell me, Lambeth, how do you go about stealing a fur coat?

Put it on and walk out.

Not even you could get away with that.

Okay, all I do is wait for a well-dressed man—you know, like a doctor or somebody—and then I walk along beside him like he's my husband. I mean, I sometimes take him by the arm so he thinks I must be a model.

And then what?

You wouldn't believe how fast I can disappear.

I'm skeptical, but never mind. What do you do with eight fur coats?

I only kept one. I'll show it to you.

What about the others?

Well, a couple of months ago I sold a silver fox because I needed the bread. I gave away the rest.

To whom?

Oh, friends. Girl friends.

What do they say? Aren't they suspicious?

Why should they be? I just tell them it was a gift from

this guy I'm not seeing anymore and I can't stand being reminded of him.

That's the most implausible story I've ever heard.

It is not. If you were a woman you'd understand.

Do you mean to tell me they're not suspicious?

Sure. But they don't ask questions.

Why have you brought this up?

About boosting stuff? Can't you guess?

No.

Then I won't tell you. Oh, all right. It was because I wanted you to know what I'm really like. I wanted you to know the very worst about me.

Why should you care? What difference does it make what I think of you?

You don't understand. I respect you. I mean, a lot.

Respect! he thinks. Respect. That's not exactly what I was hoping for. I get all of that I need. At the office. At home. Every time I walk into a bank or a shop. Anybody who dresses neatly is treated with respect. I'd rather she was infatuated with me.

Shifting gears to start up another hill he can feel the mechanism throb uncertainly; something in the metallic depths has worked loose or is about to break. Whatever it is won't last much longer and there is no sense pretending.

At the next gas station he coasts to a stop in front of the hydraulic lift. A few moments later an old man with a face like an Airedale, dressed in tennis shoes, stained baggy denims and a cheap cotton plaid shirt, comes drifting out of the shadows, chewing tobacco and grinning at Lambeth.

Muhlbach explains about the gearshift.

Foreign car, the old man remarks with an unpleasant chuckle. And then he spits very close to the fender.

Yes. It's Japanese. Are you a mechanic?

Foreign cars ain't no good.

I rented this. I need a mechanic.

Get yourself a U.S. auto. Save money.

All right, I'll keep that in mind. Do you know a mechanic?

Got a good Chevy out back. Might sell.

I'm not in the market for another car.

Good tires. Clean as a whistle. Take a look. And he points the way with his chin.

No. I want to have this gearshift repaired.

New battery. New clutch.

No.

Give me three hundred dollars.

No.

How much?

We might discuss it if the gearshift can't be fixed.

Still grinning like a gargoyle the old man spits and points up the highway with his chin. Left at the Y. Tom Stroud. Fix just about anything.

Left at the Y. Tom Stroud. All right, thank you.

Sell that Chevy for two eighty-five.

Hey, dig! says Lambeth when they are once again on the road, and she begins pointing various directions with her chin.

Stroud's garage adjoins his yellow clapboard house. His wife, a gaunt funereal figure in a flapping blue polka-dot dress which must have belonged to her grandmother, seems to have stepped out of a painting by Grant Wood or Thomas Hart Benton. In a tired voice she says there is coffee on the stove. The remark is clearly directed to Lambeth, who follows her toward the house.

Muhlbach, reflecting on this sharp division between male and female territory, follows the master mechanic toward his domain.

Tom decides after an inspection that the job could take a couple of hours. If Chick Harris got the part, he adds. If he don't, mister, you're out of luck. There ain't nothing this side of Danbury. Could be nothing there. Guess we might as well try Chick. No use paying the Danbury toll.

And having muttered something unfavorable about foreign cars he shuffles to the wall telephone.

Muhlbach listens anxiously.

Yup. Nope. Yup. Yup. Hell, Chick, I told you twice them Hercules wasn't worth nothing. Yup. Right. Nope. Thought so. Yup. Sure enough.

Tom then removes his Yankees baseball cap in order to scratch his scalp. Chick says he got it. Want to ride along?

No, I'll wait here.

Tom clears his throat, swallows, and squints at something many miles away. Pretty girl you got. Showgirl?

No.

Tom grunts, scratches his crotch with a meditative expression, hitches up his pants, and climbs into a dual-exhaust pickup with orange flames painted on the hood. A moment later he roars out of the garage.

Muhlbach decides to have a look at the calendars above the workbench.

Despite a variety of artistic techniques and the changing styles of feminine underwear the pictures look surprisingly alike. They remain dedicated to one ideal. Boneless, plump, fair of skin, untouched by the grittiness of human life, ignorant of smallpox and hemorrhoids, supremely indifferent to drought, war, pestilence and hurricane, Tom's girls ignore the march of time. It is true that the earlier ones have grown a trifle fly-specked, stained here and there by a leaky roof. And two or three have suffered the indignity of a penciled nipple. That much is true. To that extent they are not immortal.

Muhlbach studies Miss February of 1956 whose succulent haunches are clothed in pink fur, who swims languorously through a sea of bile-colored satin.

Then there is Miss September of some unrecorded year, standing on tiptoe while holding an immense oval palette and a long long brush, wearing a beret and an artist's smock which does not quite hide a pair of rosy cheeks.

And a pneumatic cherubic platinum blonde cowgirl in boots, fringed skirt and Stetson. Seated atop the old corral she winks knowingly while she blows on the barrel of a smoking six-shooter.

Fritz Willis. Gil Elvgren. Zoë Mozert. Mike Ludlow. Rolf Armstrong. Al Moore. Earl Moran. Names from the pubescent past. They are all represented. Here, too, the bulbous airbrush giantesses of George Petty disport themselves. And the rigid Varga puppets who perform their bizarre exercises with the help of hinges instead of joints.

And scattered among these—faded, curling, ripped, pitifully neglected now, often half-concealed by more recent beauties—Muhlbach discovers photographs of famous movie queens from a less disillusioned era. Betty Grable smiles persuasively across one shoulder, unaware that the Second World War has ended. Rita Hayworth in her celebrated peekaboo black lace nightgown kneels forever on the bed. Veronica Lake waits inexpressively, one eye obstructed by that metallic hair. What is she waiting for? She knows nothing of the atomic bomb, of that shocking day Truman sacked MacArthur, or of the Hungarian revolt. So far as she is concerned Korea is little more than a principality somewhere in the neighborhood of China. As for Vietnam—once upon a time Alan Ladd starred in a movie called *Saigon.*

Fascinated by the gallery of carnal masterpieces, oblivious to the fact that by leaning against the bench he has gotten grease on his trousers, Muhlbach loses himself in speculation:

Laraine somebody—what became of her? And the deep-bosomed redhead from Texas—was her name Linda or Ann or Brenda? Where is she now? Is there not something almost tragic about these evanescent symbols? The girls themselves must have lived in splendid style throughout the days of their celluloid reign and no doubt many of them are now happily obscure grandmothers. Nevertheless a tragic echo does reverberate thinly from their mission, which was to immortalize the quest for love.

Then it occurs to him as his gaze wanders up and down and across the cracked, bespattered, greasy wall, pausing affectionately at remembered favorites, noting calendar dates, that some of these goddesses flowered at a time when Tom was shooting marbles. The explanation must be that he inherited this gallery from his father or perhaps from an older brother. Well, in any case he should have the good sense to preserve these flyblown beauties and bequeath them to his son.

Sooner than expected the eminent mechanic returns, bringing a new gray-green cardboard box containing the precious gadget. But his thoughts are no longer centered on women. Maybe Chick is a football fan. Maybe there was a news item on the radio. Whatever the cause, and although baseball season has just begun, Tom wishes to analyze the strengths and weaknesses of the Jets. Joe Namath he regards as a fearful liability.

Namath? he asks with rhetorical contempt while laying out his tools. Zilch! You see the last Miami game? They out to trade the clown for somebody can throw. Plunkett. Stabler. Them guys can throw.

Muhlbach agrees.

Tom pauses long enough to light a cigar. Namath for Plunkett. How about that? That be a good trade?

Muhlbach pretends to consider. I hadn't thought about it, but you're right.

A guy can't throw, what kind of club have you got?

Not much. You don't win games without a good passer.

Bet your ass, says Tom, and trundles himself under the car. Almost immediately he reports that the left front tire has picked up a nail.

Can it be patched?

Yup, sure. I was you, though, I'd get a new one. Got one in stock. Only one that size.

Do what's best. I just hope nothing else is wrong.

Tom, dissatisfied about something, mutters and trundles himself closer to the job.

Well, I might wander over to the house, Muhlbach remarks after a few minutes. What do you suppose the women are up to?

Talking. Mopping the floor. Dishes. Busting the kids.

You sound as though you've been married quite a while. Taking everything into consideration, would you call it a happy experience?

Not bad.

Not bad, Muhlbach repeats as he walks toward the house. Not bad. There's a realist. He didn't expect a bed of roses so he's not disappointed. I must say that's sensible. That's the attitude I should have adopted before this expedition got underway. Although in spite of everything we do seem to be getting along better. I'll keep my fingers crossed. A little good luck wouldn't hurt.

Entering the kitchen is a mistake—a major mistake, no question about it. There is an almost visible stench of infant urine, cold food, floor wax, and some sort of bleach or disinfectant. Mrs. Stroud, hopelessly resigned, surrounded by an assortment of sticky brown-eyed rural children, is folding diapers at the sink. An exhausted brindle cat lies on its side in a wicker basket next to the stove, equally resigned, nursing a mewing crawling mass of kittens. Lambeth, seated on a stool, is cradling a kitten with an ulcerated eye. It seems that this kitten is a gift. And Mrs. Stroud, smarter than she looks, has anticipated every objection. She has lined a shoebox with newspaper. She has filled a plastic bottle with milk. She has filled another bottle—a tiny medicine bottle—with some kind of solution which should be dropped into the kitten's eye every few hours. And it becomes apparent that, having fobbed off the unfortunate little creature, Mrs. Stroud cannot be persuaded or coerced into taking it back.

Muhlbach at last gives up and returns despondently to the garage. The kitten will be a nuisance but what matters is the car. If Tom should decide to quit work because his wife had been offended—well, it would mean buying the Chevy. Either that or wait for a bus to New York.

So, not long before dark, carrying the bottles and the kitten in its shoebox, accompanied by an ominous flash of lightning further up the valley and a subsequent roll of thunder, they bid good-bye to the Strouds.

Scarcely have they rounded the bend when Lambeth insists on rescuing another waif—a fat mournful teenage girl in sequin-studded jeans who is seated on a log near a fruit stand waving her thumb. Her name is Deborah. She has a knapsack, a guitar, and a virulent case of acne. She is on a pilgrimage to Fedder's Hot Springs.

Having appraised this specimen of American girlhood and listened to her first words, Muhlbach can feel himself succumb to despair. The dirt, the overfed indolence, the rank East Indian perfume, the grotesque frizzled hair, the insufferable conceit—as though she were superior to those who had plucked her from the log. And the voice. A voice that could open a tin can. I just do not like this child, he tells himself. I suppose I should, but I don't. I dislike everything about her. I don't want to give her a ride. I wouldn't be surprised if she's a runaway. I don't want to get mixed up in this.

However a refusal would mean quarreling with Lambeth.

After relocating the kitten to make room for the guitar and the knapsack, Deborah wedges herself into the back seat, holding a bag of apples which Lambeth has purchased, just as the first drops of rain come pattering down.

Deborah starts to talk. She has Juju Braxton's first album. Not only that, she has met Juju. Juju signed the album.

Lambeth does not seem to know who Juju is, and Muhlbach feels obscurely pleased. She, too, is now experiencing a touch of the celebrated generation gap. But then he hears Deborah mention that she will let them see the album with Juju's name on it after dinner.

Dinner?

Deborah responds in the faintly sinister argot of her age:

Like I had sixteen dollars till I met this super dude only he didn't have his woman thing together because he beat me up and ripped off the bread.

All of which, reduced to the fundamental fact and interpreted, means that she is hoping for a free meal.

Wow! Look at this kitten's eye! she exclaims. You ought to take him to the vet. Is it okay if I eat an apple? I'm starved.

The road ahead is briefly illuminated by lightning, followed at once by thunder. A sheet of rain drenches the car.

Crazy, Deborah remarks while munching an apple. I sure do hope we get to Fedder's tonight because I lost my sleeping bag and like, man, this weather is too much.

I won't ask where it is, Muhlbach thinks. I don't care where Fedder's is, or if she ever gets there. I've had it up to the neck with this two hundred pound starveling.

I will not buy her a meal and I will not pay for her room. She's a parasite. I've seen the type often enough.

The problem, then, is how to get rid of her without antagonizing Lambeth. The rain, possibly, could be useful.

Let's see how far it is to the next town, he suggests. Driving through this storm strikes me as not only foolish but a bit dangerous. Look in the glove compartment, Lambeth. There's a map.

Lambeth unfolds the map. After considerable study she decides that they must be close to Marble Dale. New Preston, which is just beyond Marble Dale, has a black dot in the middle of the circle so it must be bigger. Also, New Preston is at the tip of a lake. Lake Waramaug.

Lake Waramaug! Muhlbach answers enthusiastically. That should be nice. All right, New Preston is where this train stops.

Deborah is not deceived. Neither is she discouraged. She comments on the storm, mentions how hard it will be to catch another ride and how long it has been since she's eaten a really good meal. But at the same time, as Muhlbach observes through the rear-view mirror, on the chance that the train will indeed stop at New Preston, she is quietly stuffing apples into her knapsack.

New Preston, regardless of the black dot, is not large. After having driven the length of the main street and searched the immediate suburbs he concludes that the Valentine motel might offer the best accommodation. The name is preposterous, the blinking red neon heart even more so, otherwise it looks acceptable.

Deborah wonders aloud if there will be two vacancies.

Muhlbach clenches his teeth. The time has come, he

tells himself. I understand that kid as well as she understands me. It's a matter of strength. If she promotes a room she'll manage to get away with supper and breakfast and God knows what else. How Lambeth is going to take this I have no idea, but it's now or never.

I seem to recall you saying you had no money.

Wow! she answers so piteously that Muhlbach almost flinches. I told you this dude ripped me off, she adds, not quite begging for sympathy yet not rejecting it, carefully projecting her image as the victim of unscrupulous friends. And he sure beat me up, she adds with just enough emphasis to suggest the horror. Like I thought he was going to do me in, you know. The big sex trip—the whole scene. It was a bummer, man. But if you want me to get out, okay.

No sooner has she stopped talking than the inside of the car lights up, thunder explodes directly overhead and a wild blast of rain obscures the windshield. So a decision must be postponed. No matter how objectionable and conniving the child may be, she must be allowed into the motel room temporarily. As soon as the storm subsides—well, perhaps by that time Lambeth will have grown disenchanted.

Twanging her guitar, Deborah lounges on the bed singing a lugubrious ballad of her own composition in a rasping adenoidal monotone while her host and hostess start to unpack. Occasionally she shakes her head with an unpleasant jerky movement reminiscent of a nervous horse, a movement presumably intended to demonstrate the depth of her emotion.

Lambeth invites her to wash, an invitation she declines.

Not only does she sing, play the guitar and compose

folk songs, she also writes poetry. At this point Lambeth, clearly afraid of a poetry recital, walks into the bathroom and shuts the door—which indicates that she won't be coming out for a few minutes.

Muhlbach, brushing his hair, begins to feel Deborah's little coffee bean eyes fixed on the back of his head. She is after something.

Aren't you old enough to get a job? he asks without turning around.

I am old enough, yes, she answers, enunciating each word. However, I am not able to work. That is why I hope to get on PDA.

What is PDA?

Public Disability Aid.

Are you disabled?

I have already explained. I am not able to work.

Why are you unable to work? he asks, staring at her in the mirror with no effort to hide his repugnance.

Deborah's eyes shine as glassily as marbles. Her smile is hideous.

Because, sir, I am not able to put up with the demands of society. If I did, sir, I could not be myself.

You're unable to put up with the demands of society?

You have heard correct. Working for somebody would be a terrific mind hassle. That is the reason I hope to get on PDA. If I do not get on PDA I must depend on friends. However, my friends do not have any money. Or I can depend on the scene.

Is that where the scene is? Fedder's?

There are some real spiritual people at Fedder's, I have been told. The karma, I have been told, is supposed to be real good there. So it will not be like on the road where you get hassled by these salesmen types.

Muhlbach reaches for his wallet. Deborah, how would you like ten dollars?

Far out, she murmurs, not giving away her thoughts. What do I have to do?

Get lost.

Man, you're too much! she answers, plucking the guitar.

Keep your voice down. Now listen to me. I won't give you another cent. This is it. If you're smart, and I know you are, you'll take it and skedaddle.

Deborah appears to be calculating. Her sallow puffy face constricts with greed.

Make up your mind, Muhlbach whispers.

You promised to buy my dinner.

Don't be ridiculous.

Lambeth did. She promised.

She did not.

You want me to go in the bathroom and tell her you offered me ten dollars?

Go ahead.

I could say you tried to bugger me.

Go ahead, you little tramp.

Why do you hate me?

Keep your voice down. I don't hate you, Deborah. I detest you. You're a leech and a hypocrite. I've seen plenty of them, so I know.

Wow! That's a heavy trip, man.

I suggest you wow yourself along the road to Fedder's. The rain seems to be letting up and with ten dollars you'd have nothing to worry about. You could find a place to sleep for that price, and if you're hungry you've got at least a dozen apples in your knapsack.

Has anybody ever told you what a dirty old schmuck you are?

Muhlbach drops the money on the bed. Deborah, I won't listen to any more insults. I'm capable of picking you up by the seat of your jeans, opening that door and dropping you in the nearest puddle, which is what I intend to do unless you relieve us of the pleasure of your company. And I don't mind saying that if you were my daughter I'd have blistered your bottom long ago.

Oh wow! I'd puke before I'd have you as my father.

You might have been better off.

Screw.

For the last time, take it or leave it. Ten dollars.

Deborah smoothes the bedspread. All at once she sticks out her tongue and grabs the money.

Muhlbach reaches for the knapsack. Permit me to help you.

Jack off, she replies softly.

Well, so far so good, he thinks, closing the door on Deborah's final gesture. Now the problem is Lambeth.

And while he waits for her to emerge from the bathroom he reflects on the progress of the trip, which could not be called a succès d'estime. Car trouble, a cat with an infected eye, bad weather, Deborah. One could be thankful, it's true, for the absence of genuine disasters such as an accident. Or the fact that the terrible child did not suddenly whip a gun out of her knapsack. All right then, what is there to look forward to?

When the bathroom door opens Muhlbach is seated on the edge of the bed with a dejected expression. Immediately he holds up both hands:

Before you say a word, Deborah has left us. She won't

be coming back. She's on the road. I don't care what you do or what you think of me, we will not go after her. Under no circumstances. Do you hear me? I refuse to discuss it. Not now, anyway. What I need right now is a drink. Then I want another drink. Then probably another. And then after I get a little food in my stomach we can discuss it. But don't say a word now. I could be dangerous.

Lambeth, having gazed at him curiously for a few seconds, merely shrugs.

Halfway through supper, with no apparent resentment, she decides to untie the package:

You must have said something while I was in the bathroom. What did you say?

I invited her to leave.

She's only a kid.

A vulture could learn a lot from that kid. She was hanging around the fruit stand just waiting for us.

Would it have bankrupted you to give her a couple of bucks?

I was not planning to mention this, but as a matter of fact I gave her ten dollars.

You mean ten cents?

Suit yourself. And treating her to supper would only have sharpened her appetite. Next she would have wanted to sleep on the couch. Tomorrow morning it would have been breakfast. Et cetera, et cetera.

Did you actually give her ten?

A liar I am not. Whatever else you may think of me, Lambeth, I am not a liar.

Muhlbach then observes a change in her expression. She does not look exactly angry, or disappointed, or humiliated. Confused, perhaps, might be the best description. Or undecided.

Is anything wrong?

No.

Quit pretending.

She went through my purse.

Muhlbach sets down his knife and fork. What did she take?

A few dollars.

When did you discover this?

Just before we left the motel.

Why did you wait until now to tell me?

She was on such a downer and it was raining and all.

But how could she have gone through your purse? She was never alone with your purse.

I don't know. I left it on the bed when I went to the bathroom. Maybe while your back was turned.

Lambeth, for God's sake, you should have told me. The only thing we can do now is notify the police.

Don't put the cops on her.

Why not?

Don't. That's all. Don't.

I doubt if they could find her by this time, but it seems to me we should tell them what happened.

I don't want anything to do with cops.

They're not going to check up on you, Lambeth, no matter what you may have done in the past.

No cops. I mean it.

As you wish, Muhlbach replies, picking up his knife and fork. You're fond of that child, aren't you? Despite the fact that she robbed you.

I guess so. She sort of reminds me of myself.

Because she's a thief?

Lambeth gestures impatiently. Who cares about that? I know where her head is.

Then you know more than I do. I haven't the faintest idea 'where her head is,' as you put it.

Nobody'd expect you to.

Am I supposed to feel sorry for that arrogant overstuffed indolent young viper? Not on your life, madam. Not on your life.

You can be so Goddamn straight sometimes you send me up the wall. You think you know all the answers. Well, I got news for you. Because you don't. You don't! You don't!

Muhlbach listens grimly while grinding pepper on the salad. Maybe it's this twenty-some years between us, he reflects, or maybe that has nothing to do with it, but for some reason we have difficulty talking to each other. I wish I knew what the trouble was. According to her I'm 'straight' or 'square,' although I certainly don't think of myself that way. And to me she seems unrealistic and self-indulgent and—well, adolescent. And occasionally dishonest. More than occasionally. But for all I know she may consider herself quite the opposite.

Karl, I want to say something. Will you please look at me?

Yes? What is it?

This was a mistake.

What was?

You know it as well as I do. And what you really want is to end it and get back to the city, only you haven't got the guts to say so.

That isn't true. I've been hoping things would improve.

You want to get rid of me.

Not at all.

You do, too! The sooner the better—I know what you're thinking.

You're wrong. You're absolutely wrong, Lambeth. But since you seem so dissatisfied perhaps we should. We'll have to stay overnight, though. Driving through this storm would be foolish. We've had problems enough already, we don't need a wreck.

You ruined everything.

Let's not throw knives. Suppose we just finish eating and then I'll look for another motel. It would be awkward to ask for a second room at the Valentine.

I don't want to sleep alone.

That's a shame.

It scares me. I can't sleep by myself.

Sorry, but you'll have to.

Hey, Karl?

Now what do you want?

Don't move out. Stay with me. Please. I'll do anything you want, only don't leave me alone.

I think that would make the situation worse. Neither of us would be able to sleep.

Yes, we can. I'll stay on my side of the bed. Oh, please! Karl listen, I might freak out.

And Muhlbach, puzzled, noticing the terror in her eyes, decides that perhaps he should agree.

At the entrance to the motel he pauses for one last breath of air. The trees are dripping and fragrant. The lake cannot be seen but its great dark presence can be sensed. Overhead most of the clouds have blown away, revealing deep reaches of the sky—glittering shards of constellations and distant luminous individuals whose very names evoke sentiments too nebulous and meaningful for the light of day: Alphard. Kochab. Regulus. Denebola. Spica. And there!—winking brightly when a cloud floats westward—shines Alphecca, fairest gem of the Northern Crown.

And while he looks at these, identifying one after another, he begins to feel a curious almost-forgotten satisfaction. No matter how the day has gone, from bad to worse or vice versa, the night sky does not comment. It is neither amused nor perturbed. It is there. It prevails.

He starts to talk about the sky, pointing first one direction and then another because it seems to him that she might enjoy learning a little:

There, Lambeth, do you see? That's Boötes, which looks rather like an ice cream cone, although in fact Boötes is the herdsman who chases the two bears around. Arcturus—that orange star at the lower point of the cone—is the only star named in the Bible, in the Book of Job. It's a giant—thirty times the size of the sun. And the Great Bear of course you know, although we usually call it the Big Dipper. See the second star in the handle? That's Mizar, an Arabic word meaning horse or steed. And just above it—half an inch above Mizar—do you see that faint star? Look just to one side and you should see it. Yes, well, that's Alcor, which means the rider, and they say that during the Middle Ages if a young man's eyes were good enough to see that star he could see well enough to join the cavalry. And do you know the name of the other stars of the Dipper? Listen. I'll start from the handle: Alkaid, Mizar, Alioth, Megrez, Phecda, Merak, and Dubhe. My son Otto, when he was very small, loved those names. He made me repeat them over and over. I wonder if he still remembers them. And now here—wait—yes, here comes the tail of Draco the Dragon out from behind that cloud! Do you see? And the brilliant star Thuban which is halfway between Mizar and Kochab. Thuban was our pole star once upon a time, about the year three thousand B.C. Now let's try to find Orion.

But Orion has gone down in the west and Muhlbach, suddenly aware that he has been talking for quite a while, asks if she is bored.

It's just that I've always found the stars exciting, he goes on before she can answer. So exciting, in fact, that when I was a kid I wanted to become an astronomer. I had all kinds of books on the subject. I thought it would be a wonderful life. I still think so. If I could do everything over I'd probably go into astronomy.

Why didn't you?

I don't know. I've often asked myself that. I suppose it just seemed impractical.

Are you sorry?

No. Well, yes. I've never been embarrassed about what I do for a living. There's nothing shameful about the insurance business and it's rewarding in certain ways. Nevertheless, there have been occasions—oh, I don't know, Lambeth. I do feel a little thwarted, which must sound ridiculous. I shouldn't have mentioned it. Tell me, when you were a child what did you dream of doing?

I wanted to be a nurse.

A nurse? I'd never have guessed that. Never.

Yeh, I pretended I was wearing this white uniform with a red cross on the cap and I went around taking the temperature of all these guys that had been wounded on the battlefield. It was real crazy.

Did you give any serious thought to becoming a nurse?

Sort of. But you know how it is. I mean I started going with this guy. He was a photographer . . .

She continues talking but Muhlbach no longer listens. The moon is down and in the starlight, in the shadow of the trees, she is almost invisible. We've never been so close, he thinks. My God, I'd forgotten what it was like to be close to anybody. I haven't felt like this in years. Not since Joyce and I were first married. I didn't know I could ever feel this again. I thought it was too late, but maybe it isn't. We're so close I don't dare move. I'm afraid to touch her.

And it seems to him while he stands next to her in the darkness with the rain dripping from the trees all around, hearing no other voice, no other sound, and her face illuminated by the starlight—it seems to him that this is where he belongs. In this place, at this hour, with this woman. Yes, this is how it was meant to be. Everything is logical and right. Yes, we should be here, he thinks. And we can solve the problems and live together. There's no reason we can't. I thought it would be impossible but it isn't. This astonishes me. I never imagined it happening. She needs me, I see that now. Why was I so blind? But that doesn't matter. Nothing matters anymore except that now I understand. She's had a terrible life. She's young and she's had to put up with so much, but I know how to help her. That's what she needs. It may take time but we have plenty of time.

Then he becomes aware that she has stopped talking. Evidently she has nothing further to say about being a nurse and she has heard enough about the stars. Her feet are wet. She would like to go inside.

Muhlbach unlocks the door and holds it open until she has crossed the threshold, then follows her inside and bolts the door against whatever perils might unfold in the dead of night around Lake Waramaug.

Lambeth kicks off her shoes. She tosses her raincoat over a chair. She pulls out another cigarette, coughing at the sight of it, sits on the edge of the bed and picks up the telephone. She would like to call New York.

Muhlbach concludes that he may as well go into the bathroom and spend a long time brushing his teeth because she looks as if she intends to chat a while. It would be awkward to stand around pretending indifference and even more awkward to lie down beside her on the bed. The only alternative, except the bathroom, would be to step outside again.

Lambeth makes no attempt to speak confidentially.

Hi, Jarv! It's me, doll. Your voice sounds funny—have you got a cold? Listen, you'll never guess where I am. Lake Waramaug or something like that. Crazy, huh? Yeah, I know. I'll explain when I get back. Well, I couldn't. I mean I couldn't, sweetheart, you'll just have to take my word for it. Yeah, sure. No, of course not, I think about you all the time. What? I can't hear, babe. You what? Oh! Hey, great! Listen, sweetheart, I just called 'cause I wanted to let you know how much I love you. No, I'm fine. I got kind of bent out of shape, that's all. It was a bad scene, you know. I mean really. Hey, Jarv, I do love you. No kidding. I can't wait to see you.

Muhlbach observes himself in the mirror stolidly brushing his teeth and decides that the events of the day must have paralyzed his face. It no longer looks or feels capable of reflecting any emotion.

Having rinsed his mouth and hung the toothbrush in the cabinet he looks around for something else to do, because Lambeth is still talking. He inspects his fingernails, which are trimmed and clean. He examines the tip of his nose for blackheads but can find none. He explores his bald spot, wondering if a program of scalp treatments might be helpful. Or there is the possibility of transplants—although somehow that smacks of self-glorification more than a natural regard for appearances.

At last, because she is now exchanging long-distance kisses with Jarv—presumably Jarvis, presumably the Jefferson City podiatrist—Muhlbach seats himself on the stool and slowly polishes his glasses. While he gazes at the shower curtain he tries to excuse her behavior. In the first place, being that time of the month, she's tense. In the second place she probably feels humiliated by the encounter with Deborah. After all, to be robbed by somebody you have befriended isn't much of a compliment. Then there was the car breaking down—that long delay. She was imprisoned for almost three hours in a kitchen that smelled like an Assyrian compost heap. Each of these factors no doubt has contributed. She is overwrought. Even under the best of circumstances she could not be called a model of stability and reason. She has a singular tendency to go berserk. But still, in spite of everything, it's inexcusable. Just unbelievable, he thinks, shaking his head. I absolutely cannot believe this. I cannot under any circumstances imagine myself doing to her what she is doing to me. How is it possible to be so unconscious of another person's feelings? Or maybe she knows, but doesn't care.

All at once Lambeth taps on the door. Whenever he is through with whatever he is doing she would like to take a bath.

Muhlbach jumps up and opens the door. Why not a bath à deux? That is, ensemble. In other words—because it appears that she does not understand—how about sharing the tub?

No.

You loved it the other time.

Yes, but things have changed. Go watch television.

So there is nothing to do but capitulate. Either that or seize her by the throat. And I can't, he thinks while hanging up his clothes. If I had Antonio's guts I would, but I can't. He wouldn't stand for this nonsense, he wouldn't listen to a word she said, he'd grab her and they'd be floundering around on the bed by now. But what am I doing? Hanging up my pants.

The brown plastic box flickers and hisses. Snow falls diagonally across the screen. Distorted nightmarish figures lurch to and fro. At last, however, the magic device collects itself and Muhlbach crawls into bed.

The bed seems damp.

After feeling about with his fingers he concludes that the moisture is restricted to one area, which would indicate a leak in the roof. He looks up. Yes, the ceiling is discolored. But it has stopped dripping, which, under the circumstances, might be regarded as the best news in quite a while.

With a sullen expression he stares at a commercial on the screen and thinks about that splendid bath in her apartment—the iridescent bubbles and the perfumed water and her marvelous salamander body. Yes, that was a bath to remember. Yes indeed. For sheer sybaritic indulgence it would be hard to beat. Nor will it be forgotten. As the philosopher said, some mindfulness a man should keep of anything that pleased him once.

Then it occurs to him that she has neglected to lock the bathroom door. Could this be regarded as an invitation? Probably not. Probably she just didn't bother. On the other hand, because women are fundamentally and obstinately devious, an unlocked door cannot be dismissed. One can't be sure. It's worth thinking about.

All at once the water stops thundering into the tub and he waits expectantly, prepared to interpret the slightest noise. But there follows only an idle plashing which cannot be construed as anything more than it is.

Karl? she asks in a melodious voice. Are you awake?

The question could be answered several ways. But what's the use? Why make an effort to be amusing, sardonic, inscrutable, or anything else? Yes, I'm awake.

What are you doing?

Watching a movie.

Aren't you furious?

No.

You are! I can tell from your voice. You feel like strangling me.

Not necessarily.

What did you say?

Nothing.

Behave yourself. Pour the kitty some milk, I bet she's hungry. I saw some cups and saucers on that shelf underneath the coffee gadget.

How would Antonio handle this? he wonders. And having filled a saucer with milk he stands with his arms crossed while he watches the kitten and tries to imagine how Antonio would react. Taking into account the unlocked door, nothing could be more obvious.

But the threads of half a lifetime are not easy to break. Inconspicuously yet very effectively he has been tied down—day by day, month by month, year after year. This is incredible, he thinks, I can't move! And he looks around with a feeling of desperation. And everything in the motel room confirms his fear.

The telephone cord attracts his attention and at that moment he hears a ripple of water, so Lambeth must be sitting up.

Karl?

Yes?

Don't come in! I mean that. I don't want you in here. Stay out.

She's afraid of me, he thinks. In fact she sounds terrified.

Suddenly he discovers that he is inside the bathroom looking down at her. In the blue water, motionless, she resembles a Bonnard painting. Fascinated, he watches a drop of water trickle across her breast. Then a gust of wind rattles the bathroom window and all at once he cannot remember what he had intended to say or do. He looks away.

She picks up the washcloth and a bar of soap.

Why don't you run along to bed? You must be really exhausted.

No, he thinks, I'm not exhausted. Or maybe she's right. I can't decide. I feel confused.

I broke in on you. I'm sorry.

Okay. No big deal. Now you run along to bed. If you need a sleeping tablet look in my purse.

Much later, after having arranged himself like a question mark in order to avoid the damp spot, he feels the mattress tilt slightly as she creeps into the bed and curls up, not touching him yet near enough that he can smell the lotion on her hands. And before long her breathing proves that she is asleep.

Sometime during the night he opens his eyes to find the motel room suffused in a supernatural blinking primrose light. The explanation, however, is simple: just across the road the Valentine's fluorescent neon heart is industriously at work beckoning late travelers. The storm seems to have passed. Lake Waramaug is quiet except for the distant quacking of a duck.

Presently he becomes aware of a subtle intense noise very close by. Unable to believe what he is hearing or to locate it he turns his head on the pillow and as he does so a passionate muffled gasp indicates that the invisible lovers are indeed very near. In fact, if it were not for the wall, which apparently is made of cardboard, it would be possible to touch them.

One partner, the man, soon drops out of the contest. Snoring can be heard. The lady, however, to judge by the creaking bed, is restless. She mumbles to herself, coughs, goes to the bathroom for a drink of water, flushes the toilet, and returns to bed. But still she does not go to sleep.

Muhlbach asks himself what might happen if he tapped on the wall. Would she understand? And if he should whisper, explain that he too was being left out, how would she respond? Suppose a shameless proposal were offered. Mademoiselle . . .

But I can't, he thinks, lying with a despondent expression on the edge of the damp spot. I'd give anything if I could. Why can't I? Antonio wouldn't hesitate. He'd tap on the wall. He'd be out of this room and into that room like a flash. He wouldn't care about the danger. Why should I? My damned Lutheran heritage, that's why. All my scruples. All that middle-class training—O Lord, it dangles around my neck like the albatross. Why have I been condemned to worry about consequences?

He turns his head to consider Lambeth, who has slept through the neighborly performance without a quiver, and it occurs to him that she might be able to sleep through anything. The flashing red neon heart intermittently reveals the solid egg-shaped mound of her hips.

After contemplating this shape for a while he lays a hand on it. She is not disturbed.

He feels compelled to draw closer. He lifts himself on one elbow in order to study her face. Without his glasses though, particularly in this stroboscopic light, she is only a seductive blur so he plucks them from the night table and after having hooked them around his ears he scrutinizes her. The lips, the skin, the alluring column of her throat. On the pillow, like a disorganized golden spider web, the pale skein of hair. And it seems to him that in the mysterious depths of sleep she somehow has been able to comprehend his desire because her small mouth gradually opens as though anticipating a kiss. Yes, she understands.

But she continues to breathe with deep solemn regularity, suspecting nothing, and her face glows with such a look of adolescent innocence that he cannot bring himself to do what he intended. As softly as possible he kisses her cheek, hoping that in her dream she will mistake this for the kiss of a handsome prince.

THE next noise he hears is the plaintive note of a harmonica, and almost at the same instant he becomes conscious of sunshine on his right hand. So the night, the surrealist night, must be over. Lambeth is not in bed nor in the bathroom. But her suitcase is on the rack, which means she hasn't run away. She might have gone to the motel office for a newspaper.

Without enthusiasm, because the day doesn't offer much except an interminable drive to New York, he swings his feet to the floor and stands up, only to learn that he has acquired a stiff back. The wet mattress probably is responsible but the cause is unimportant. Supporting his back with one hand, grunting and wincing, he hobbles toward the bathroom.

After having washed his face he straightens up cautiously and appraises himself in the mirror. Morning is not the best time. Morning sunshine, for some inexplicable reason, tends to make one's hair look gray. Almost silver. It does not look as gray as this in New York. And the shattering brilliance reflected from Lake Waramaug seems to magnify every wrinkle and pouch.

Disappointed by what he has observed, for he had supposed that just the opposite might be true—given the fresh Connecticut air—he proceeds with his morning ritual. And before long he hears once again that grieving all-but-forgotten sound from the irretrievable summers of childhood. Somebody is indeed wailing away on a harmonica.

Puzzled by this lugubrious concert, especially at such an hour, he steps to the window.

At the edge of the lake, ankle-deep in water, stands the provincial musician—a graceful young man perhaps twenty years old with an abundance of black curls and a beard befitting Methuselah. He is attired in a sun-bleached work shirt and dungarees which appear to have been hacked off at the knee with a blunt instrument. He has, at least from this distance, a face which could almost be mistaken for that of a goat. As might be expected, his poignant serenade is aimed at Lambeth.

Wherever she goes a man is certain to pop up. It never fails. They materialize with the infuriating assurance of dogs, which is perhaps inevitable, but what is astounding is how quickly they are able to divine her presence.

Having inspected his jowls and decided that shaving can be postponed until after breakfast, having combed his hair and polished his glasses, Muhlbach drops the room key into a pocket of his coat and goes out to investigate.

The name of the new conquest is Saul. Saul lives in a

nearby cabin. He cultivates vegetables and eats no meat, not so much as a chicken. He salutes the sun each morning, he meditates and he plays the harmonica and that seems to be about the extent of his activities. He used to paint, sculpt, write, and dance, but now he has achieved a higher level of awareness. Lambeth is impressed.

Muhlbach, doing his best to look not unfriendly, stands around listening to their conversation, thinking about breakfast and resting his back from time to time by leaning forward with his hands on his knees as though he were studying a colony of little frogs. He observes how Saul stands with the magnificent ease of youth—one leg bent like Michelangelo's *David*—and thinks of how agile and limber and tireless he himself used to be. Perhaps an hour of exercise several times a week might restore that elegant youthful sinuosity.

The boy is pleasant enough, that much must be granted. He is courteous, with a gentle voice, and seen close up he does not look exactly like a goat. In fact he gives the impression of a shallow-water bird, a half-grown undernourished crane. His shirt, unbuttoned to the waist, reveals a torso like a washboard. He is far too thin, no doubt because of the stringent diet. He is so thin that he is almost transparent. Maybe he is an illusion. Soon he will glide across the surface of the lake playing his harmonica.

But Saul at last says good-bye and wades around the point like any other man. And then for quite a while, until the bleat of his instrument can scarcely be heard, Lambeth praises his wisdom, his sensitivity, his beauty, and the fact that he does not devour innocent animals.

Muhlbach, sick of hearing about Saul, asks bitterly where they all come from.

Where does who come from? Are you jealous? she asks, laughing and patting him on the cheek. Then she hops up on a fallen tree and starts to walk along it, waving her arms for balance. Wouldn't you love to go someplace, Karl? I mean someplace where we could spend a lot of time together. Wouldn't that be neat?

She hops off the other side of the tree and runs through the bushes toward a little beach. Muhlbach follows slowly, clutching his spine, grateful that she does not turn around. Away from the road there is hardly a sound except the occasional lap of water, the crunch of footsteps, and the twitter of birds. The sun has risen high above the oaks, the breeze is warm. Now and then a fish breaks the placid surface.

I want to get to know you, she remarks when he has caught up. We've got so much to tell each other. We're practically strangers, she adds, staring across the lake. We shouldn't be strangers. I mean, it's foolish. Don't you agree?

Eight hours ago you were pledging yourself long distance to what's-his-name.

Jarvis is a doll, she replies with a thoughtful, positive expression. But I get tired of boys. Don't you understand?

No.

She sighs impatiently. I want to know everything about you. I want to meet your children. I want them to like me. I want to see your place—where you sleep and eat and that green leather armchair you talk about where you like to read. And I want to meet your horrid Mrs. Grunthe. Why do you keep her on?

I have no idea, Muhlbach answers, wiping his forehead. I guess because I'm afraid to give her notice.

You told me you had a townhouse with a little garden. Can we have lunch in your garden? I'd like that. No kidding.

So would I.

Will Mrs. Grunthe serve us?

She might condescend.

And will the neighbors' Persian cat sit on the wall and watch?

Unless it's raining, yes.

Will your children like me?

Otto will be destroyed.

And what's your little girl's name again? Oh, I remember. Donna. Will she like me? Or will she hate me?

I imagine she will be fascinated.

And you've lived there a long time, you said. Can you see the river?

From upstairs, yes. From the bedroom I can see at least three hundred square yards of river water.

And yesterday when I asked if you could love me you wouldn't answer. Why not?

I wish I knew.

Don't you think you could?

I'm not sure.

What if I was rich? Not just rich, you know, but super super-rich.

I would succumb immediately, Lambeth. Immediately.

Well, okay then. Listen, this may be a shock, but I guess now is a good time to tell you. My last name isn't Brent.

Muhlbach looks at her curiously because she has stopped smiling. He decides to attempt a little joke—perhaps something about Natasha Petrouchka, the long-lost great granddaughter of Czar Nicholas, heiress to the crown jewels—something of that sort. But as he looks at her serious face he changes his mind.

Who are you? he asks. If you are not who I think you are.

You won't believe me.

Tell me anyway.

If you promise not to laugh.

I've never laughed at you. With you once or twice—not as often as I'd like—but never at you.

Okay, she replies after a deep breath. Here goes. You've heard of the Svensen Steamship Lines? Well, Axel Svensen is my father. My mother's name was Erica Branch. She was a dancer but they never got married so he can't acknowledge me. It would be bad for the company image. I haven't seen him in years. At least ten years. He used to visit the Brents late at night in this huge old limousine. I'd hear him talking in the front room and then he'd come into my room and ask how I was doing at school and if I was minding Mr. and Mrs. Brent. I remember being just absolutely amazed at how tiny he was. He's sort of a dwarf, you know. Oh, hey! Why not sit down? she asks, pointing to a log. You probably want to rest. You look like you had a terrible night. I guess that was my fault.

Seated next to her on the log, letting the sun warm his

spine as he picks thistles out of his socks, Muhlbach reflects on the possibility that she might be telling the truth. It's not probable but it is possible. Her story sounds too bizarre to be a lie. How much simpler to concoct a plausible lie—some variation on the wealthy uncle in Australia. Or Grandma's will which has been tied up in litigation. Could Svensen be her father? That grotesque confrontation in the bedroom, then trying to stab her mother with a bread knife—or was she referring to the Brents? In either case, did it happen?

You two would get along great, Lambeth remarks with a dreamy smile. I'll find out when he's going to be in New York. I mean he travels a lot and of course he lives in Sweden, but maybe all three of us could have lunch together.

Perhaps we could. Tell me, do you resent the fact that he doesn't publicly acknowledge you?

No, because he's got a point. I understand how it would be bad for the company.

Do you often see your mother?

My mother? Oh, I guess I forgot to mention it. She's been dead a long time. She was killed in a plane crash in Luxembourg.

You said her name was 'Erica Branch'?

Yes, she was a soloist with the Stauffer Dunn ballet. Everybody said she would have been famous if she'd lived.

Well, thinks Muhlbach, a little research would show us if there actually was such a dancer. If not, that's that. If so, then what?

She danced all over Europe, Lambeth continues. I've

got pictures of her. I'll show them to you sometime. That's why I studied ballet, but I didn't have much talent.

Are you the only child?

He told me I was. But I don't know. He's such a funny man.

I understood you had a sister and a brother. Someone at the Christmas party mentioned it

Oh, you mean Judith and Mickey. They're the Brents' kids. Of course everybody thinks the Brents were my parents, so naturally they think we're related even if we don't look alike. You're the only person I've ever told about this. You've got to promise not to tell anybody else.

All right, I won't say a word. Now I'm curious about something, Lambeth. Do you realize what this could mean?

About inheriting his money? Sure. Why do you suppose I told you who I am?

She picks up a pebble and tosses it at a frog.

This is preposterous, Muhlbach thinks, gazing past her at the lake rippling in the sun. Trying to relate to this girl is like trying to catch up with somebody in a hall of mirrors.

Well! he exclaims, putting his hands on his knees. We should get some breakfast and start back. We've got a long drive. Now how about the kitten? Are you planning to keep it?

No.

By the way, where is it?

She answers in a sullen voice, her face averted. It ran off. I don't know where it went. You said we could spend three days in the country. I don't want to go back to New York. I want to go driving some more.

Muhlbach stares at her, struck by the thought that she may have drowned the kitten. She seems oddly evasive, almost defiant. In fact there is something very nearly menacing about her in a shallow infantile way.

You do as you wish, he replies, getting to his feet. Explore the countryside from here to Fedder's Hot Springs if you like, but I'm eating breakfast and after that I'm heading south.

You said you wanted to spend the whole weekend with me.

I did. I did very much. But somehow that seems like a century ago.

Why did you change your mind?

Because I've had all I can take of your perversity. Suppose we leave it at that.

You said you loved me.

Don't be ridiculous.

What's ridiculous about loving me?

Muhlbach hesitates, then begins slapping the dust from his trousers.

All at once Lambeth darts off the log with a shrill cry and goes running and skipping along the edge of the lake while he watches in astonishment. But just as suddenly she stops and comes walking toward him with her head down, pretending to study the beach.

Hey, she murmurs without looking up, and comes to a stop in front of him. I want to go away with you. How about it?

No, I'm afraid we can't, he answers while brushing the dust from his hands.

Why not?

Because it would be impossible.

Put your arms around me.

After a moment, because there seems to be no reason he should not, he does so.

Just what I thought, she remarks.

What do you mean?

You love me all right.

Do I?

I feel it in your body. You love me so much you don't know which way to turn. You're a mess. You're more screwed up than I am.

On the highway approaching New Milford, calmly filing her nails, not having said a word for half an hour, she again brings up the subject of Axel Svensen.

You don't believe he's my father. You don't, do you! Okay, here. Look at this.

She pulls a bulging red leather dime store wallet out of her purse, unsnaps it and extracts a frayed scrap of newspaper.

Muhlbach, after a glance into the rear-view mirror, quickly reads it. Under the headline 'Tycoon in Hospital' there is a photo of Svensen. The item states that according to a company spokesman the sixty-eight-year-old Svensen has been admitted to a private clinic in Zurich for treatment of an undisclosed illness. Associates refuse further comment, et cetera. No mention is made of a daughter, no reference of any sort which could establish a relationship, yet Lambeth seems to regard the article as proof of her claim. Why? It proves nothing.

Now do you believe me? she asks, and carefully folds

the scrap of paper and returns it to her wallet. And if that's not enough suppose I show you a copy of his will. I've got a copy in my trunk.

Let's not have another argument. If you say you're his daughter, all right.

I'm going to inherit everything he owns.

Congratulations.

As soon as he dies I'll be able to buy anything. I could buy the whole bloody fucking Riviera.

Just about.

I could buy your Mickey Mouse company.

Lambeth, if you don't mind . . .

And whether it is because of the request or some other reason she subsides.

Nearing the city, as they are about to enter the tunnel, she looks at him shyly.

Hey, listen. Would you—I mean—oh shit, forget it! Take me home.

MONDAY morning at the office Gloria reports that there was a phone call on Friday afternoon from a Mr. Rafael López y Fuentes.

All he said, Gloria continues while scratching her scalp with a pencil, was it was important and you were supposed to call him. Anyhow here's the number. So now let's get down to business. I want to hear about the red-hot weekend.

The weekend?

How'd it go? Whoopee all the way?

Let's just say it was instructive.

That's all you're telling me? What am I going to tell the girls? Here you are topic A and they say 'What happened, Glo?' and I say 'Well, he said it was instructive.'

I'm 'topic A'?

Sure. What'd you expect? Everybody's talking about nothing else.

Has Mr. Hammersmith said anything?

Not that I heard. Want me to check?

No. No, of course not.

Bad scene, huh? Gloria asks, eyeing him shrewdly. You should've invited me.

Perhaps next time.

I'm gonna remember, says Gloria, winking and crossing her legs.

López y Fuentes, evidently anxious to talk, calls again and suggests that they meet for lunch.

I'm afraid this may sound blunt, Muhlbach responds, but why should we?

Because you will not be sorry, in my opinion. As a matter of fact I will go so far as to say the opposite. My friend, believe me: to have lunch will be to your advantage. I give you my word.

Riding the swivel chair in a narrow arc, irritated and at the same time rather curious, Mühlbach asks himself what López could have in mind. It must have something to do with Lambeth, there couldn't be any other reason. Does he suspect I'm warming half of her bed—the bed he used to occupy? But even if that were the case what could he be up to? Does he want me to intercede on his behalf? In the first place, assuming I could help the man, which I can't, why should I? I'd be the last person to approach. This makes no sense. None whatever. Nor do I see any point in having lunch with him.

López, however, is not easily discouraged.

No, Muhlbach replies with more emphasis, and brings the swivel chair to a halt. Aside from our mutual acquaintance I'm afraid you and I have very little in common.

Exactly. Yes, very little, López agrees. Then for the third time he proposes lunch.

Displeased and uncomfortable, Muhlbach cannot decide. López obviously is hinting at something.

Today would be impossible.

No, no. It should be tomorrow.

What does he mean 'should be'? Maybe nothing. Difficulty with the language. And yet the construction sounded deliberate, as though he knew exactly what he wished to say. As though he had selected just the proper nuance. Tomorrow. For some mysterious reason they must meet tomorrow.

Very well. I could make it around one o'clock.

En punto, yes.

I may as well let you know right now that my afternoon is fully booked. Our lunch will have to be brief.

Yes, yes.

Where would you like to meet?

López suggests the men's bar at the Biltmore.

Remembering the apparition on 53rd Street, Muhlbach hesitates. It would be embarrassing if not impossible to meet somebody who was in that condition at the Biltmore. He might not be admitted. Or he might do something peculiar—collapse or start waving his arms and shouting. And another neurotic confrontation would be the final straw. My God, he thinks, I've only begun to glue myself together after that nightmare in Connecticut.

López prattles along with his usual cultivated inanity:

As goes without saying you are to be my guest. If you please, there is to be no argument, none. I will not hear of arguing. It will be for me a great pleasure to see you again. And to be the host. Is this agreed?

As you like.

Bueno! Until tomorrow, eh?

Until tomorrow.

Or as we say in Honduras: Hasta luego. Which does not mean especialmente 'tomorrow.' In other words, very soon. But you understand, do you not?

I do.

Adiós, caballero.

At thirty minutes past the hour, drumming his fingers on the bar, looking with distaste at the Western paintings on the wall, Muhlbach is about to empty his drink and walk out when López y Fuentes briskly descends the steps—neat, crisp, freshly shaved, beaming like a TV huckster, eager to shake hands, bright-eyed, fashionably dressed, fragrant with cologne, manicured, oiled and burnished from top to bottom.

But the explanation is simple. The earth is a horn of plenty. In other words, aren't there more young girls than anyone can count? Or to express it another way, does a hungry man walk through an orchard without plucking a little fruit?

So you've found somebody else? Already?

López settles one foot on the brass rail and snaps his fingers at the bartender. Then he is ready to elaborate.

Permit me to say that what you suppose to be true is true, yes. I will not deceive you. As for what is past, that doesn't concern us. To worry about yesterday—how foolish, eh? Life does not go on without one day coming to a stop, as we know, of course—when, like ourselves, you and I, if you do not mind my saying so, we have reached a certain age. It will come to an end, life. It will be kaput, no? Fini. Terminado. It's too bad, but that's how things are. In consequence, my friend, if you do not mind me referring to you in this way, it has occurred to me that it would be wise to take the bird in hand.

That's all very well, but unless I'm mistaken you were utterly obsessed by Lambeth. You were practically disintegrating.

This may be so.

Yet already you've recovered—as though she were nothing but a temporary indisposition.

Yes. Permit me to explain.

Please do.

It is because she does not possess that quality without which the most beautiful woman in the world becomes undesirable.

And what is that?

It is the quality which we call 'compasión.'

I'd have to agree.

So, in a word, I'm happy to be rid of her. I'm much happier now.

You do appear to be.

Very much, let me assure you. I'm in love.

You weren't in love with Lambeth?

López feigns amusement. He taps the side of his head. I could tell you a couple of things which would astonish you, my friend, and it's possible I will. But on the other hand possibly not, I don't know. I'll have to think. But I can tell you this much because I am now happy: Cuidado! That is to say, look out!

Yes. Well, Muhlbach reflects, he's a bit in arrears with his advice, I no longer need to be warned. And as for all this trumpeting about happiness—I've got my doubts. He might be covering up.

López, if I sound cynical you'll have to excuse me, but I must admit I find your dramatic change of heart rather startling. To say nothing of the change in your appearance. The last time I saw you, unless I'm thoroughly mistaken, I thought I was looking at a ghost—a man without a shadow. If you don't mind a somewhat lurid figure of speech, it was as if Lambeth had sucked your blood.

This is true. Because you have not been in love, Mr. Muhlbach. You know the little papers which will change color in water?

Litmus?

Yes. So in the same way, let me remind you, does one appear differently when one is fortunate enough to be in love.

I agree. But I hardly need to be told about that. I was married for a number of years.

All the same, amigo mio, you know nothing about love. Nothing.

Don't be absurd, Muhlbach snaps. Now what's the purpose of this get-together? We won't have time for lunch because I've got a two o'clock appointment.

I am late and I wish to apologize. Everybody is supposed to be on time. It's my fault. Excuse me, I'm sorry. Now we will get to the heart of the matter, if you like.

The fact, I am happy to say, is that I am no longer without a position, which, as you may guess, also contributes very much—oh yes, very much indeed—to my happiness.

You got a job. Is that what you mean?

Yes, you have put your finger on it. But I am able to see by the expression of your face that you do not believe me. You believe otherwise, and that it is my wish to take advantage of you. I would like to assure you such is not the case. I have, in fact, found a job.

Good.

Yes. Permit me to tell you about it.

I don't have time. Congratulations. I'm pleased that you found something. And now I must get back to the office.

One moment! One moment, eh?

What do you want?

You believe that I have invited you only in order to discuss myself, is this not so? Yes. But this is not the case. Not at all. Permit me, my friend, to ask. Are you, by chance, acquainted with the film company Aphrodite Films?

No, I am not. You mentioned at Dolly's party that you were interested in filmmaking. You said, as I recall, that you hoped to become a Hollywood producer.

That is my hope. However, one step at a time.

Yes. And now I really must say good-bye.

You have a two o'clock appointment, I understand. However I believe you will not be sorry to cancel this appointment.

Muhlbach, prepared to walk away, looks down at López with an annoyed smile. Cancel an appointment?

For what? Then he remembers that Aphrodite Films was in the news not so long ago. Some sort of legal dispute. Civil liberties—police—what was it? Ah! Ah hah! Yes indeed. Aphrodite was the outfit making pornographic movies. They were all arrested—the entire bunch. Or was it only the projectionist? Or the theater manager? In any case it doesn't matter. So López has gone to work for these people, has he? Well, well. But what has that to do with canceling an appointment?

Muhlbach studies the patient friendly deceptive Latin face—those amiable brown eyes as brown and engaging as the eyes of a squirrel or a deer, the smooth tan skin, the sensual red lips, the brilliantined hair, the precise, impeccably trimmed Xavier Cugat mustache. What does this amiable little person want? What's his game?

And suddenly the fog begins to lift. The fog lifts, revealing the swamp. One way or another Lambeth has gotten mixed up in this business.

López y Fuentes, perceiving that his message has been deciphered, goes on as agreeably as ever to explain that the rushes of Aphrodite's newest spectacle will be shown to a small group of friends this afternoon. And what are 'rushes'? Simply a technical term referring to a working print of the film. After watching the rushes the filmmakers decide which scenes should be cut, which should be reshot, et cetera. In other words, although this film must not be regarded as a finished work of art it should be interesting. Claro?

Muhlbach nods.

Now permit me to say, López adds with the sleek certainty of a Bible salesman, that you will not want to miss *Double Honeymoon* because I can assure you beyond doubt that you will not be able to believe your eyes. Lopez then lowers his voice. Fantástico!

And for a little while he pretends to be occupied with his drink, allowing time for the implications to sink in.

Muhlbach, feeling rather light-headed, picks up a coin from the bar and puts it down again. I don't dare go see that thing, he says to himself. What if I got sick at my stomach? But if I don't—if I refuse—my God, I'd spend the rest of my life wondering.

So there appears to be no way out. What should be done?

With a thoughtful expression he empties his drink. He clears his throat. He frowns at his watch.

Tell me, López. This, ah, this film, how long would it last?

López does not answer immediately. His eyebrows angle toward each other. He spreads his hands. At last he responds:

Twenty minutes. Thirty minutes.

Muhlbach attempts to register surprise. Oh? I guessed it might be longer.

López then explains that films of this type usually are short in order to prevent the customer from becoming bored. After all, who cares to watch the same girl do the same thing for two hours? Consequently a theater might book half a dozen little movies. Maybe a dozen.

To round out the program, so to speak.

Yes. And some, you know, are very short—oh, five minutes. Peliculas pequeñitas.

Not very much dramatic motivation, in other words. Just five minutes of gymnastics.

That's right.

By the way, this job of yours. What do you do for these people?

After the usual circumlocutions what it comes down to is that López has been hired as a publicity agent, messenger, goodwill ambassador and talent scout. But you would be surprised, he adds, as I have been, to discover how many beautiful young girls would like the opportunity to make an appearance in one of these films produced by our company. I assure you, it's amazing.

You're not serious! You can't be.

All day the telephone rings. All day, my friend, I'm not joking. They have heard that Aphrodite will be making another movie. They request the opportunity to come over to the studio in order to reveal what they look like.

Aphrodite must pay a great deal.

To the actresses? Not very much, no.

In that case why are they anxious to appear in your films? Certainly there must be better ways to earn a living. Or do I sound naïve?

Yes.

Yes? Muhlbach wonders. What does he mean? That I'm naïve? Or that I'm right about better ways to make a living?

López, tell me. Just exactly why do these girls want to be in a film?

López, wearied by such innocence, can only sigh. His eyebrows move toward each other until they almost touch. He flicks a mote of dust from his sleeve.

Because they are women. They are not like us, you and me, eh? Life, in the opinion of women, is merely a lot of bodies, that's all. Now let's step on it, we're going to be late.

You're sure this wouldn't take more than twenty minutes?

López has grown impatient. Twenty, thirty, forty—who cares!

All right, but I've got to phone the office.

In the booth while waiting for Gloria to check the afternoon schedule it occurs to Muhlbach that he does not feel quite like himself. All of my senses seem a little dead, he thinks. How strange. I must be a bit frightened. But of what? Of what I'm about to see? Yes. The idea scares me. But I'm sure I can stomach it, no matter how repulsive it is. I've been exposed to these things. Not for years, but I remember what they're like. That preposterous business with the Arab—it's been twenty years since I saw that. And the one with the dogs. And there was one with some burlesque queen, I've forgotten her name. So I should be able to get through this. Except for Lambeth. My God, I don't know, maybe I shouldn't. But on the other hand why should I care? Her Sunday 'appointment'—why try to deceive myself? I know what she is. And calling that kid from the motel, telling him she was alone while I stood there brushing my teeth. I just wonder how long it's been since she showed anything that could be mistaken for common decency. Quite some time, I'd guess. And to think I was infatuated. Incredible! Apparently I'm not as sophisticated as I thought. But at least I've got enough sense to admit my mistakes. Small comfort, I suppose. Just the same it could have turned into a bona fide disaster. Now what's keeping Gloria?

Ah! There you are . . .

Gloria reports that Mr. Nye has left a message. He will be fifteen minutes late. He was two o'clock, she adds around the chewing gum. And then Mr. Rosenberg—I guess it's Rosenberg. I can't read my writing.

Nye, Muhlbach says to himself. What a stroke of luck. And he's going to be late. Everything should work out. Gloria, listen. I expect to be a bit late myself. Let's say half an hour. Mr. Nye is an old friend so he won't give you any trouble. Now what time is Rosenberg?—assuming it is Rosenberg.

Two forty-five.

Very good. I'll try to be there by two-thirty.

Is this the same one?

Is what the same one?

The one you went on the weekend with? I'm just curious.

No, this is a different one, Muhlbach adds after thinking about it. And I don't mind telling you confidentially that she's gorgeous. Exquisite. Gloria, I'm at a loss for words.

Oh yeh? No kidding! She sounds terrific.

That's right. Furthermore, she has a quality which I find most endearing. Can you guess what it is? Don't answer because I intend to tell you anyway. She keeps her nose out of my business.

Oh, Gloria replies after a pause. Oh, Mr. Hammersmith just called so I better see what he wants.

That sounds like a splendid idea. Kindly give Mr. Hammersmith my regards.

Yeh, sure. I mean, okay I will. And as soon as Mr. Nye comes in I'll tell him you expect to be a few minutes late.

Excellent. Excellent, Gloria. Now if I might bid you adieu . . .

During the crosstown ride López never once refers to Lambeth, although he is not reluctant to discuss his new position, despite the size of the cabbie's ears. He explains in excruciating detail the singular problems, the necessary subtleties, the perils and the benefits of working for Aphrodite.

Muhlbach, arms folded, gazes out the window with what he hopes the cabbie will interpret as an air of experienced boredom.

López winks. He lays a finger beneath one eye in that unforgettable Latin gesture. He talks volubly, enthusiastically, explaining why certain actresses are chosen. He summarizes the plots of various scripts under consideration. He details the sexual idiosyncracies of his employers. He pats Muhlbach on the knee in order to emphasize their mutual masculinity.

Nor does he shrink from describing with clinical precision the anatomy of his new love, Ingrid, one of the starlets in Aphrodite's constellation of beauties. Ingrid is sixteen years old and what a figure! Que chichas! Que nalga! And is she passionate? López answers his own question by flapping one hand as if he had burned himself on a stove.

Sixteen? Come now, López, you're exaggerating.

I assure you, my friend. Sixteen. Yes.

You could get into serious trouble.

López, however, cannot be intimidated. What's life without a pinch of danger? A meal without salt, that's what.

The cabbie, who has not missed a word, ratifies this gem of folk wisdom:

Etsda troot. Okay, guys, heewee ah.

Aphrodite's top executives have assembled in the screening room—up a dismal echoing mahogany-colored flight of steps off Seventh Avenue, a flight of steps that in better days, to judge by an occasional bent tack, must have been carpeted.

The screening room, too, whatever its original function, has witnessed more gracious times. A chandelier hangs from the ceiling, a glittering queenly crystal apparatus perhaps made in Europe. Now it reigns over a sterile whitewashed crypt decorated at one end by the screen and at the other end by the faintly ominous projector. The two windows of this room, handsome windows that once upon a time opened on a pleasant vista, are nailed shut and painted black. Everything is functional. Cheap and functional. Collapsible metal chairs. An ugly if serviceable table and a still uglier imitation leather couch. Dented rusty film cannisters. Dime store ashtrays. Scratch pads. Pencils. A hot plate, a jar of instant coffee, powdered cream, a cylinder of Dixie cups. No expense had been authorized that could be spared.

Muhlbach, hoping for anonymity, reluctantly finds himself introduced to Marty the director and Hughes the producer—both in their middle thirties, youthful veterans of the West Side struggle for existence. And to Sam, the money man, who could be mistaken for an old Jewish sheepdog.

Then, after having established himself as comfortably as possible on a Salvation Army chair, he looks around at his companions, the chosen few. It is difficult to see them through the layers of smoke. Sam's friends—beyond doubt Sam's friends—gray, bald, paunchy and soft, rather like cheese blintzes behind their shell-rimmed glasses, seem somewhat more repulsive than the younger movie fans. But that, of course, is an illusion. There's no difference. Twenty years from now the friends of Hughes and Marty will look just as disgusting. And how many of them, old or young, have spent a night, or an hour, or a few minutes in Lambeth's bed?

Muhlbach begins to feel trapped and slightly nauseated. He considers easing out the door, flowing down the steps without a sound and melting into Seventh Avenue. But he knows he will not do this. He has come to see the movie. Squeamishly, less with anticipation than apprehension, anxious to get through it quickly, hopeful that it will not last twenty minutes—nevertheless he has come to see it.

But what if somebody in this crowd should recognize him? What if the children found out? It might not mean anything to Donna, she's too young. But Otto—that would be a different story. Or suppose Mrs. Grunthe learned of it. Yes, that would be still another story. And Muhlbach imagines himself at breakfast pretending to read the stock market report while Mrs. Grunthe serves ham and eggs. Ah, so you've fallen on your face in the gutter, have you? Filthy films now, is it, sir? Didn't I always suspect you were no good? You're no good, I say! You're no good! No good!

Hughes and Marty are enthusiastic about their latest effort. They expect a heavy sale. Hughes delivers a little speech. He is convinced that with a smart distributor and a few good notices in the right spots this picture should gross more than *Junior Prom,* which earned ninety thousand. In Hollywood, of course, that kind of money won't even get you the script, not a first-class script, but ninety thousand ain't to be sneezed at. For a skin flick it ain't bad. And this baby could do ten times that. Hell, who knows? Twenty, thirty times that much. It's a winner, so everybody spread the word.

The glittering light from the chandelier is turned off. *Double Honeymoon* starts to unwind:

A distant shot of mountains, very possibly the Catskills. Next a resort scene. A station wagon drives into view with JUST MARRIED spray-painted on the rear window. The station wagon parks in front of a cottage. The newlyweds get out and begin to unload luggage. The husband, dressed like a small town sheik, is comically awkward. He staggers toward the cottage trying to carry four suitcases, a golf bag and a tennis racket while his bride follows, daintily carrying a hatbox. He attempts to open the door without putting anything down. She waits behind him, graceful and demure, swinging the hatbox, gazing at the mountains. One suitcase drops, then another, the other two, the racket, the golf bag, and then, predictably, the groom himself falls down. The bride pretends not to notice. The groom awkwardly picks himself up, rubbing one elbow. He dusts his pants. He scratches his head. At last he manages to unlock the door and he carries the suitcases inside, one after another, while she waits on the threshold with a petulant expression. He is puzzled that she does not come in. He scratches his head again. He frowns. Oh! He smiles knowingly, then she smiles. He picks her up, carries her inside. Before putting her down they kiss. Her shoes drop off, her toes curl.

At this point the film begins to flicker and a curious

ticking noise can be heard. Hughes reaches for the light. Marty goes to work on the projector. Sam thoughtfully unwraps a cigar.

In a few minutes the problem has been solved.

The bride and groom unpack. In addition to golf clubs and a tennis racket he has brought along a swimming suit—an old-fashioned striped suit with shoulder straps—a baseball mitt, a casting rod, a set of dumbbells, and an elastic muscle-building device which he tries out—breathing deeply, admiring himself in the mirror. The bride has brought clothing. Negligees. Slips. Quite a number of black lace items and shoes with impossibly high heels. She studies a nightgown at arm's length, shakes her head, pouts, drops it and picks up another. Meanwhile the groom practices with his tennis racket, anxious to get on the court. Now the bride, presumably searching for something on the bed, leans over while the camera zooms in on her plump hindquarters. The groom, astonished and delighted, flings the tennis racket aside and starts toward her. But just then somebody knocks at the door. Who could it be? He glances at his bride, whose expression is intended to signify alarm. He goes to the door, opens it cautiously and registers amazement by slapping himself on the cheek. On the threshold stands another new husband ready to carry his bride into the cottage.

The second bride, poorly disguised under a brunette wig, is Lambeth.

Ay! murmurs López with a cold and bitter smile. Vaya la puta! Ay cabrona! Tu quieres joder?

The actors discuss this unfortunate situation. The second husband, having displayed a key, argues that the cottage belongs to him. Yet the first husband also has a key. How could such a mixup have occurred? The brides stare at each other contemptuously while the camera goes over them from top to bottom. The first husband has an idea. He picks up the telephone. The manager of the resort will settle this question.

But at the opposite end of the line the manager—Hughes, wearing Bermuda shorts, sandals and a Mets baseball cap instead of tailored slacks, loafers and turtleneck—Hughes the resort manager shrugs eloquently. Every cottage is occupied.

The camera holds for several seconds on a No Vacancy sign.

Inside the cottage the four newlyweds, unable to resolve this embarrassing probem, decide to have a drink. Bottles are brought out of suitcases. An ice bucket is opened.

They drink. They stare at each other. They drink some more. One of the husbands loosens his tie.

The camera holds on a clock while the hands move swiftly around the dial to prove that an hour has passed.

Now everybody is more relaxed. Lambeth's blouse is half-unbuttoned. The other bride begins pulling the pins out of her hair, shaking it loose. The first husband lights a thin brown hand-rolled cigarette and inhales luxuriously. Marijuana. He passes it around. All of the participants inhale, holding the smoke with desperate determination while they exchange significant glances. The first bride yawns, delicately patting her mouth. Her husband pretends to stretch.

Ahora? López inquires with deadly sarcasm. Vamos a culear, eh?

The newlyweds decide this might be a good idea and before long the screen is awash with breasts, thighs, mouths, buttocks and the genitalia of both sexes. *Double Honeymoon* concludes in a monumental tangle of prostrate motionless bodies followed by a close-up of the No Vacancy sign.

Hughes snaps on the light.

López, having exorcised his demon, gives Muhlbach a brotherly pinch on the arm. I am sorry. I believe I know how you are feeling at this moment, if I may say so. But I have said to myself that for you to see this picture—that would be the best thing.

Muhlbach nods.

Permit me to offer a little advice. Find another girl, eh? Because this one—well, she doesn't like herself.

Muhlbach, afraid to speak, nods again.

Entiende, caballero?

Yes.

Listen, my friend. This girl was to me, as the expression goes, the only girl in the world. So perhaps you will understand how angry I became with myself, of course, when it came to my attention that she is like this. A little whore. Una puta.

Muhlbach discovers that he has gotten to his feet. López also stands up.

Adios, amigo. Take care, eh? In other words, don't do anything you will regret. Because I can assure you it will not be long before you have forgotten this girl. You'll be surprised, I give you my word, how easy she is to forget. And now permit me to wish you good luck. Suerte.

As he goes down the steps Muhlbach admits to himself that he had been concealing the truth. I was still in love with her, he thinks. I pretended I wasn't, but now I feel the ache. It's like a bad tooth. I'll be all right, I know I will. But I do hurt. O Lord, I hurt.

Suerte, he murmurs, pushing open the door to the street. Yes, I could use a little luck.

It occurs to him that he should telephone the office to let Gloria know he will not be coming back for a while, but the idea of talking to anybody seems intolerable and he decides to walk through Central Park. By the time I get to the other side, he tells himself, I should be in control of the situation. At the moment I'm destroyed. I feel completely helpless. I doubt if I could tie my shoe. It might have been kinder if she'd just shot me in the stomach.

And while walking through the park he attempts to organize his thoughts, which seem to be flying in as many directions as leaves in a storm. Why did she do it? For the money? López said they weren't paid much. What other reason could there be? Is it true that she's nothing but a whore? Maybe she was forced to put on that show, wriggling and grinning and arching her body like an eel. The drugged smile when they went into her, one right after the other . . .

Walking resolutely through the park, fingers knotted at the tail of his coat, he reminds himself to be careful. Yes, that was good advice. Cuidado. Don't step off the curb and get hit by a bus. Keep your eyes open. Don't do anything stupid. The pain won't last forever. Keep going. Keep walking.

Yes, I can keep myself moving, he reflects, but how can I quit thinking about her? That will be the hardest part. I can force my body to do whatever should be done, it's the mind that won't obey. Well, I won't see her again, I know that much. That may be all I know but I do know that much beyond a doubt. Never. If I should meet her accidentally I'd pretend I didn't see her. No, I'm not able to do that, no matter how I detest a person. I'd speak. But I wouldn't stop. I may be a fool now and then but not such a fool that I'm incapable of learning. So this much at least is clear—she and I are through. And good riddance. And I hope López was right, I hope I forget her very soon.

Maybe I haven't been hurt as much as I thought, he tells himself a few minutes later. Just walking through the park seems to help. The trees and the grass, everybody enjoying the sun—yes, I'm beginning to feel better. I'm shocked, of course. Jolted might be more accurate. I wasn't prepared for one or two of those scenes. It's not easy when you know the actress. Lord, how vile she is. I wonder if she got López involved in that sordid business or if it was the other way around. Well, it doesn't matter, I doubt if I'll see either of them again. I hope not. Although it was decent of López to do what he did. He went through the crucible a second time. Or did he do that for his own benefit? It was almost as if he enjoyed the degradation. I wouldn't put it past him. His behavior certainly was odd. He might still be in love with her. God knows she's deadly.

And so at last, unable to stop tormenting himself, Muhlbach emerges from the park not far from the museum and looks around for a telephone.

Gloria reports that Mr. Nye, who was supposed to arrive almost an hour ago, has just come in. Mr. Rosenberg, not due until two forty-five, arrived early, got impatient and marched out saying he would do business with a company that knew how to maintain a schedule. Mrs. Costello from Hanover Trust, whose appointment is not until three-thirty, is already in the office. And Miss Cunningham called. And there's a conference at four.

No. No, says Muhlbach to himself, I'm not up to it. I thought I was all right but I'm not.

Gloria, listen. I'm not feeling well. I won't be back to the office this afternoon.

Gee, that's too bad. What am I gonna tell Mr. Hammersmith? I mean about the conference.

Tell him I'm sick. I might go home, I'm not sure. I can't seem to pull myself together.

You do sound funny. Did you drink too much at lunch? That always does me in.

No, I had very little to drink so please don't start a lot of rumors. Did you say Mr. Nye was there?

Yeh, I'll put him on. Do you want Miss Cunningham's number?

No.

She said it was an emergency—ha ha!

I'll give her a call just in case it is an emergency. Now let me talk to Mr. Nye.

Hi, sport! Nye exclaims, chortling. Gloria tells me you put away too many martinis at lunch.

Hello, Chet. No, the truth is I got some bad news. I feel rather twisted out of shape. I'll get over it, but at the moment I'd be a liability at the office. Can we make a date for the first of the week?

You bet. I'll have my girl work it out. By the way, congrats to Hammersmith.

What did you say?

Congratulate Hammersmith. Gloria tells me he's been elected to the board.

Oh. Oh, yes. That's right. I'll give him your regards.

Karl, you sound damn strange. Where are you?

Near the Met.

The Metropolitan Museum of Art?

Yes.

What are you doing there?

It would take a while to explain.

I bet it would. I just bet it would. Look, tiger, how long since you had a vacation?

I don't feel like talking, Chet. We'll get together next week. Give my love to Kate and the children.

Sure thing, sport. Heads up.

Yes. Good-bye, Chet.

And now, he thinks, squeezing his lower lip and frowning, what else was I supposed to do? There was something else. I can't seem to keep myself in focus. I feel tired. I'm not nauseated but I feel as though I could sleep for a month. What else? Ah! Eula.

I should scold you, Eula begins with the mock anger she customarily employs to show affection. I must say you are the most despicable man I have ever known. But I've decided to be sweet, aren't you lucky? Now for heaven's sake don't tell me about your trip because I'll refuse to listen . . .

And she goes on talking until Muhlbach interrupts:

Eula, please. Is there something important?

Oh my goodness! Her laughter skips along the wire. I should say there is! I've discovered the most divine recipe for lasagna with mushrooms and I can't wait to try it out. Doesn't it sound delicious? Now I insist you come over this evening, do you hear? I insist!

I'm sorry, Eula. Tonight, no. I couldn't.

What on earth is the matter with you? Have you been drinking? Your voice is slurred. Are you all right?

I don't feel well.

Tomorrow, then. I'll expect you for supper tomorrow.

I'm afraid not. I'm sorry if I sound rude. You'll just have to excuse me.

A week from tomorrow?

Mrs. Grunthe is going to visit her sister sometime next week. I'm not sure which day, but I don't want to leave the children alone.

You can't keep making excuses, you beast. A week from Friday. You've nothing planned that far ahead because you never do. Unless you promise right now I'll camp on your doorstep. No, I'll visit you at the office and tear my blouse and rush around shrieking. So give me your answer at once.

All right, a week from Friday.

Eight o'clockish. Oh, how I despise you! What a dreadful man! Don't be late.

Muhlbach shrugs and wanders away from the telephone. Nothing seems important. Supper with Eula or not, it doesn't make any difference. Nor can he make up his mind what to do with himself for the remainder of the afternoon.

Presently he realizes that he has been shuffling along the sidewalk like an outcast—head down, hands in his pockets, dragging his feet. He makes an effort to stand erect. And there in front of him is a museum poster:

UKIYO-E

Nineteenth Century Japanese Woodblock Prints

Pictures of the passing world. Fuji. Edo. Hiroshige's little people caught by the elements. Utamaro women with mirrors. Geishas. Actors. Swordfights. Well, why not go inside? Anything to fill up the afternoon.

Climbing the steps, depressed and exhausted, he wonders how long it will take to forget the movie. Or will it ever be forgotten?

And as he goes through the film once again in his mind he is struck by how foolish it was, how unimaginative. Stereotyped characters, ludicrous symbols. And how curiously asexual. Not in the least provocative. Why do Concerned Citizens get upset about such films? A naturalist's documentary of copulating chimpanzees might be more erotic.

But if I felt no sensual excitement what did I feel? he asks himself. Aside from Lambeth being in the thing I can't say that I felt much except boredom. Mild disgust, perhaps. No, I'm not even sure of that. Contempt would be more accurate. The script was so puerile. Boredom and contempt. Well, here we are. Ukiyo-e.

At the beginning of the Edo period a new mode of painting which depicted the customs and events of everyday life, treated in a realistic and straightforward manner, became popular in Japan. Widespread dissemination of these works of art became possible after the invention of xylography, or wood-block printing, generally credited to Hishikawa Moronobu (1618–94) who was born in Boshu, Chiba. Arriving in Edo in 1658, Moronobu began to illustrate the activities of commoners and their pleasure district, the Yoshiwara . . . Moronobu's technique was subsequently improved by Harunobu . . . Other popular wood-block artists such as Shunsho, Toyokuni, Shigenaga, Kiyonobu, Kyosai . . . influence spread throughout the world, clearly evident in the works of James McNeil Whistler . . . principles of linear perspective focused on a central point . . . coarse absorbent paper composed of thousands of interlocking fibers into which the ink has been impressed result in vibrant . . . flowing line, bold yet poetic . . . additional color blocks . . . a world which the beholder, circumscribed by the limitations of individual vision . . .

Wandering down the corridor, sometimes standing on tiptoe because of the crowd, Muhlbach loses himself in the magical pictures. He stops in front of an emperor at the seashore who seems to be anticipating the instant when a crane will unfold its wings—an instant taut with expectancy.

And here is the great Ichikawa Danjuro, his features striped like a Sioux chief.

Here are several Eishi ladies fervently praying for rain.

The green-gowned geisha Itsutomi, her lute resting on the floor. Does she remember or does she wait?

And here, inevitably, are the Utamaro women. Only one, really. That one whose beauty pervaded his brain and guided his fingers over and over. Obsession? Was there ever a man more obsessed by a woman than Utamaro?

And, of course, those battered little travelers of Hiroshige. When the snow lets up, if ever it does, what vicissitudes will greet them on the opposite side of the bridge?

Nishimura Shigenaga viewing cherry blossoms at Ueno Lake.

Masanobu's puppeteer.

Sukenobu's courtesan dressing her hair.

Kiyohiro's busy evocation of love at Dojoji temple. How much time and thought has been consecrated to love.

Saharku actors. Saharku himself reputed to have been a Noh actor. In less then ten months he created one hundred and forty sets of actor portraits, then he vanished. Even today we do not know what became of him.

Three Kiyonaga ladies cooling themselves at Okawa riverside.

Another band of travelers. The rain slants down furiously. How absurd they look beneath their flimsy straw umbrellas, torn by the insensate wind. How pitiful they are, yet how tenacious. On and on. One step, then the next.

Nakazo as Hotei.

Views of the Tokaido road.

Foreign warship.

Li Po admires a waterfall.

Girl with mouse.

Geese descending at Katata.

Doll festival.

Fuji from Hodogaya.

And one more perfect beauty—this one mincing along beneath a yellow parasol, extravagantly costumed, coiffed and painted. As artificial as Lambeth fitted out for public consumption in a wig, high heels and Copenhagen striptease underwear.

Pictures of the passing world. Yes, Muhlbach reflects, I should say so.

Outside the museum, hands in his pockets, eyes fixed

on the pavement while wandering toward no particular destination, he asks himself if she might have been drugged. That would explain quite a bit. Her curious unnatural smile. Her languid sensual movements. And her apparent willingness to do anything. Very possibly she was drugged. Not that what she did could be excused. But still . . .

Looking up, he discovers that he is not far from where she lives and it occurs to him that there could be no harm in walking past the apartment.

I won't stop, he tells himself, that's the last thing on my mind. I certainly don't want to see her again. I'll just walk by as though I happened to have business in the neighborhood. As a matter of fact that might do me some good. One last glance at the place might help me resolve my feelings. If I were in love with her it would be foolish—suicidal—but I'm not. Not now. Her body—that's all it was. López, though, evidently he failed to perceive the difference. Which is odd, considering how experienced he is. And the result was that she almost wrecked him. Not that I haven't deluded myself, but at least I understood the situation sooner and quite a lot more clearly than he did.

Halfway down the block to her apartment is a delicatessen.

Inside is Lambeth. She is wearing new Levi's with a flower embroidered on the seat, a bleached sweatshirt and a kerchief which gives her a remotely Russian aspect. She appears to be studying an avocado while listening to a garrulous young fop in a brown corduroy jacket, turtleneck sweater and trousers cut from a pizza parlor tablecloth. His hair, fitted like an ivory helmet, seems to have been styled after the Frankish knights and a pair of sunglasses perched on top of his head like a visor suggests that he has been competing in a tournament. But whoever he is, his progenitors did not sit at the king's right hand because the blunt muddled face and the vulgar loquacity indicate a more common bloodline.

At this moment a rat the size of a cat streaks out of the delicatessen followed by a yelping slavering black-and-white blur which could be a fox terrier. And Muhlbach in mid-stride, passing the open door, unbalanced by one or possibly both animals squirting through his legs, after having set a foot on something slippery, flings up both arms as though he had been immensely surprised and skids into a display of peaches. Not that this matters, nor the fact that in contriving not to fall down he has wrenched an ankle. A few squashed peaches aren't important. And the ankle, which has begun to expand and contract, transmitting fluorescent currents of pain—the ankle eventually will take care of itself—tomorrow, next week, next month. What does matter is that Lambeth along with everybody else in the delicatessen and half a dozen of those marblehearted fish-faced commentators who materialize at each public disaster—Lambeth, curious about the disturbance, still holding an avocado, has recognized him.

She starts for the door.

Muhlbach, attempting to smile, waits for her to arrive by standing on one foot.

Now get this, she begins in an unpleasant voice. Lay off. I mean that.

He looks at her in dismay because it seems to him

there has been a misunderstanding. When she got out of the car at the end of the trip she had been almost affectionate. In fact she had brushed his cheek with her lips.

It's over. It's over, she repeats, and the sound of her own voice makes her angrier.

What are you talking about? he replies. What are you saying?

Get lost! Get lost! she hisses, thrusting her face at him.

He begins to explain that he just happened to be in the neighborhood and had not expected to see her, but with every word her rage increases.

Please, Lambeth, he continues, hopping closer, let's not argue. I want to talk to you. If I've said something to offend you I apologize.

Don't touch me, she answers in a tone that he has not heard until this moment.

But what's wrong? Can't you tell me what's wrong?

Just then the young fop arrives with a bag of groceries, wearing a smile fit for a pumpkin. He introduces himself:

I'm Jarvis O'Reilly, Mr. Muhlbach. Lambeth has told me a lot about you, sir. It's a pleasure to make your acquaintance.

Muhlbach glances at him with hatred but the boy will not retreat. Smiling and unconcerned, he stands on the sidewalk like a plowhorse.

Sir, he announces, I want to tell you how grateful I am.

What? Did you say 'grateful'? Is that what you said?

Yes, sir.

Baffled by this remark, offended at being treated with

such deference, Muhlbach glares at him. The boy is as common as a loaf of grocery store bread. Despite the à la mode clothing and the tinted glasses and the twenty-dollar haircut—despite these caste marks which are meant to imply Continental sophistication—Jarvis O'Reilly is a product of the very midst of middle class America. To judge by his accent and his manners he must be the pride and joy of some Missouri dry goods prince or druggist who doubles as treasurer of the Kiwanis Club. Jarvis himself, no doubt, played high school football. He has the build of a tackle with the untroubled countenance of an Eagle Scout. To think that he might ever speak disrespectfully of his parents is inconceivable. He has not shot dope, he has not mugged anybody. He is remembered affectionately by his neighborhood theologian. At Christmas he receives a box of homemade fudge and a warm sweater from the biggest department store in town. So here is Jarvis O'Reilly, forthright and upright, unabashed and presumptuous and convinced of his value, Horatio Alger in New York to seek his fortune.

Good God, Muhlbach murmurs to himself, she'll eat this kid alive. He won't know what happened.

Lambeth, taking her docile escort by the hand, leads him away. He permits himself to be led, glancing across his shoulder once like a friendly inquisitive bulldog.

Muhlbach watches them zigzag through traffic, Jarvis clutching the groceries, and after being very nearly run down by a truck they dash into her building as happily and innocently as Hansel and Gretel.

I don't understand, he says to himself. What does she see in him? Not that early American honesty. And he's not handsome. No, in fact he's quite an imperfect specimen. His right eyelid droops, and apart from the eyelid he's no Adonis. Broad, swaybacked, masculine without being conscious of his masculinity, beefy, amiable, slow to anger, neither foolish nor brilliant, with thick ruddy freckled hands good for chopping wood or skinning pigs, Jarvis is the fruit of generation after generation of Celtic and Saxon tradespeople. A substantial decent boy, yes, but not one to inspire passion.

So it seems to Muhlbach that before long she will call. Tomorrow or the next day she will call. She will apologize. She will mention that night at the lake when they stood so close together looking up at the constellations. Or the fresh morning when sunlight glittered on the water and birds flickered noisily through the trees. Or the time they went to see Antonio. And she will admit that she has begun to get a little tired of the pride of Jefferson City.

EACH time the telephone rings, at the office or at home, he feels both apprehensive and relieved and before accepting the call he reminds himself that she should be the one to apologize.

But the week ends with no word from her and the following week ticks inexorably along toward Friday—Friday and lasagna with Eula—while he goes about his duties masked by an air of thoughtful dignity just as though his vitals were not being devoured.

Then, while he is in the bathroom, less than an hour before he is expected at Eula's, Otto pounds on the bathroom door.

Yes? What is it?

Mrs. Grunthe said to tell you Miss Brent called.

Muhlbach answers as soon as he is able to trust his voice: All right. Thank you, son.

Otto does not go away. He wants to know who Miss Brent is.

Miss Brent is a friend.

This does not satisfy Otto. You told me Miss Cunningham was your friend.

That's right. Miss Brent is another friend. But this isn't the time to discuss it. Have you finished your homework?

Practically.

Which means you haven't started. Suit yourself, but you know the rules. No TV until homework is finished. Now I'm serious. And he turns on the shower but then turns it off because Otto is still talking.

What? I couldn't hear you.

Otto, affecting unspeakable boredom, repeats his message. Mrs. Grunthe said to tell you Miss Brent said to tell you to call her up right away.

Why didn't you say so in the first place? Did she leave a number?

Otto isn't sure.

Go ask Mrs. Grunthe. And step on it!

Otto returns with the information that Miss Brent did not leave a number, which means she must be at home.

All right, my good man. Thank you very much.

You sound like you got a screw loose.

Ah ha! I do, do I? Muhlbach asks while quickly putting on his robe. Well, maybe I have. What would you say to that?

Otto walks away mumbling.

As a matter of fact I probably do, he repeats half aloud as he hurries toward the phone. If I had any sense I wouldn't talk to her. Hah! So she called! I knew she would. She must have been feeling guilty all this time, which is why it took so long. Yes. Yes, of course.

However Lambeth does not sound guilty. Certainly she is not repentant. She is drunk. Abusive, almost incoherent, thoroughly drunk, and as vulgar as her undistinguished imagination permits. Muhlbach, not daring to interrupt, listens unhappily to her catalogue of pointless obscenities and insults while squeezing the tassel of his robe.

I ought to hang up, he thinks. I can't stand this. I've got to get away from her. And he begins walking back and forth as far as the telephone cord allows.

Lambeth's witless denunciation flows monotonously across the wire with the repugnant uniformity of sewage. She laughs brokenly. In the background something crashes as though she had either dropped or thrown a glass. Then she begins to shriek. But almost at once she stops.

After a long silence she resumes in a sober voice:

Hey, listen, aren't you going to come over? I want to see you. I really do.

All right, he answers, shutting his eyes.

Okay, hurry. Don't fuck around.

En route to her apartment, slumped in the back of a cab as though he were riding in a tumbrel, sick with dismay, appalled at what he is doing and occasionally twisting his fingers, it seems to him that he cannot escape. I can't help myself, he thinks. This is grotesque, I'm going the wrong direction. I should be on my way to Eula's. I ought to turn around. All I've got to do is tell the driver.

But he cannot bring himself to sit up and tap on the glass.

Well, he continues, I should call Eula. Lord, she'll be furious and I don't blame her. There was a phone outside that delicatessen. I'll do it from there.

Then it occurs to him that Lambeth might not be alone. Now wouldn't that be dandy, he thinks, biting his lip. Suppose somebody's with her. She's capable of a stunt like that. In fact she might be capable of blackmail. I'd better keep my eyes open.

In front of the delicatessen after a glance at his watch he jumps out of the cab.

Eula is delighted to hear from him. She was about to dash across the street to Victor's Market for a bottle of Chablis.

Now Karl, she exclaims, do be an angel and pick it up. I'll tell Victor to expect you. But you're not to pay. Absolutely not! Victor will put it on my account. You never dreamed I had a charge account at a liquor store, did you! See what you've done? Now don't be late because the lasagna smells divine. Oh! I interrupted. That's one of my worst habits, I simply can't control my tongue. What did you start to say?

After having delivered his message Muhlbach waits, but instead of recrimination he finds himself listening to a profound stillness. He begins to wonder if they have been disconnected. And then from infinitely far away he hears a strain of tremulous echoing laughter.

Eula, he begins when the laughter has subsided. Eula, I want to make this up to you. Why don't we go someplace special one evening soon?—maybe to The Colony for supper. Or, since you enjoy dancing, we could try one of the big hotels—perhaps the Waldorf or the Plaza. How does that sound?

But this only sets her off again. I don't understand the joke, he thinks, frowning. But I wish she'd get over it. I'm late already. My God, I was afraid I'd never find a cab.

Oh! Oh, she gasps. You poor dear! Oh my! Excuse me, Karl, this is just too funny.

And with that she is off again.

Would you explain? he asks when she seems to have recovered.

Yes. Oh yes, I do owe you that much. Goodness! Oh my! Pardon me while I blow my nose. This has been simply too much. Now what were you saying?

I'd like to know what amuses you.

Oh Karl, you can't be serious! Don't you know? Honestly, don't you know? Of course you don't, how silly of me. Heavens above, I haven't laughed so much since I was a child.

I can't understand a word you're saying.

Well then, you'll simply have to excuse me. I'm being giddy again—the same old Eula you've always known. Isn't that so? I've always been scatterbrained, haven't I? Even before I gained all this weight you thought so.

You're talking down to me.

Am I? You're right, I am. Well, my dear, how long have we been acquainted?

Quite a while.

A long time, wouldn't you say?

Yes.

We began to see each other after Joyce died.

Yes. What are you getting at?

And I began to tell myself that you'd learn to care for me. I told myself so often—night after night—until I actually convinced myself. I persuaded myself that you and I and the children might have a life together. Now you must admit that's amusing.

Not in the least.

Forgive me, but I think it is.

Eula, there dosn't seem to be much point to this conversation. I feel awful about breaking the date, especially at the last moment, and I keep trying to apologize but all you do is ridicule me.

Dear Karl, I suppose you're right. You almost always are. It's just that when I think of—oh my! My poor sides!

I'll talk to you again soon.

You'll talk to me again? Is that what you said?

Obviously you don't believe me. But I do want to make it up to you.

How typical! And how sweet. Good-bye, my dear.

Good night, Eula. I'm sorry.

You weren't listening. I said 'Good-bye.' Oh, she adds theatrically, adièu! Farewell! I did love you, Karl Muhlbach, even when I hated you so much that I was ready to scream. And now good-bye good-bye good-bye.

She couldn't have meant that, he says to himself while hurrying across the street. Although she did sound rather emphatic. Well, I haven't got time to analyze the situation.

In front of Lambeth's building he stops long enough to adjust his necktie and take a deep breath of the humid poisonous city air. Then, before approaching the entrance, he glances up. The windows of her apartment are dark, which is odd. Could she have stepped out for a minute? If so, why bother turning off the lights? But there's no sense speculating.

He presses the worn white button beside her name.

After a while he presses the button again.

Finally he walks across the street in order to get a better view of the windows. She could be there, of course, waiting in the dark. But why didn't she answer the bell? It doesn't make sense. What about telephoning? That wouldn't accomplish much because, after all, if she is inside and for one reason or another refused to open the door she certainly wouldn't answer the phone. She must have stepped out, that's the only explanation. All right, waste some time by walking around the block and try again.

So, after having wandered around the block, gazing at various shop displays and pausing frequently to consult his watch, he returns to the door. But still the lights are out and nobody answers the bell.

It occurs to him that he could get a bite to eat, which would use up half an hour. She ought to be back by then. Yet even as he attempts to convince himself that nothing is wrong, that there has only been a misunderstanding, he knows she is gone. With her customary disregard for everyone else she may have gotten tired of waiting and run off to spend the evening with Jarvis. On the other hand something disastrous could have happened. She might be lying upstairs in a puddle of blood, although this is hardly probable.

Just then he notices the patrol car. It has coasted to a

stop not far away. Both officers are studying him. One of them beckons.

The interrogation is not dramatic, nevertheless it begins to draw spectators. The street had been very nearly deserted but suddenly it is alive, and there are faces at every window. So the thing to do is justify one's self as rapidly as possible. Get out of the neighborhood before somebody arrives with hot dogs and programs. Get out once and for all. Yes. Yes! he thinks with astonishment. That's what I want. Why didn't I realize it?

When they permit him to leave Muhlbach can hardly withhold a sigh of relief.

And that's that! he tells himself. No more. That wasn't good night, Lambeth—that was good-bye! I never thought I'd feel grateful to the police for sweeping rainbows out of my head but they certainly did. I saw myself for the first time in quite a while and I won't pretend I liked the picture. As Veach said, she'd have taken me down so far nobody would have heard the splash.

On the way home he tries to remember how the affair started. At La Galette, of course, although actually it began at the party. Or before that, on the bus. When she sensed me staring—that was when we first became conscious of each other. And now it's finished. Kaput. Terminado.

Yes, it's over, he repeats aloud while opening the door to his house. I'm sorry, but thank God it's finally over. I don't know what possessed me. A generation between us, to say nothing of the gulf between our temperaments. I must have been out of my mind. Everything I did seemed natural—sending roses, that disastrous Connecticut idyl and so forth. If I'd known the girl in February I'd probably have sent her a satin-covered heart-shaped box of chocolates. I was sailing downstream all right, faster than I imagined, and the rapids weren't far ahead. I really ought to mail those cops a box of chocolates.

After having exchanged a few sociable comments with Mrs. Grunthe in the kitchen, meanwhile eating a cold turkey leg in order to give the impression that nothing unusual has occurred, Muhlbach decides to find out what his children are doing.

Donna, ready for bed, is groggily following a television drama. Another few minutes and she may be asleep on the sofa. Will she give her father a kiss?

How I needed that! he thinks while walking along the hall to Otto's room. All the king's horses and all the king's men couldn't do as much for me as she can. I'll be all right. I'll recover. I have my children, my house, my job, and pretty soon I'll glue the fragments of my head back together. There's nothing to worry about.

So what is Otto up to? Ah ha! The stamp collection! And he's busy cataloguing some new treasures. At the moment he is testing a violet three-cent Washington against the perforation gauge. There should be twelve perforation marks, according to the description in the album, however something seems to be wrong because there are only ten. Otto is peeved.

Maybe the stamp belongs on a different page?

Otto insists it does not. It goes on this page. In this spot.

Muhlbach looks thoughtfully at the perforation gauge. Not because he is concerned about Otto's problem but because the gauge has stirred a few memories.

He himself had used this gauge when he was Otto's age, just as he had turned the smooth creamy leaves of this same thick beautiful blue album.

With Otto's reluctant permission he picks up the album just to feel the weight. It is every bit as heavy as it used to be. And as comforting to hold. And he thinks that someday when Otto is not working with the collection he will turn through the pages again to see what other memories might be evoked.

Before returning the album to the table he glances at the flyleaf. There is the bookmark, pasted in thirty years ago, still quite fresh. *This Collection is the Property of . . .* followed by *Karl Muhlbach* in the graceless calligraphy of a schoolboy who did not pay much attention during penmanship class. And the picture on the bookmark—a lithograph of a serious collector, a pair of tweezers in one hand, a magnifying glass in the other—yes, how familiar that is. Only one thing about the bookmark is different. Otto has updated matters. He has drawn an authoritative line through *Karl Muhlbach* and beneath it has scrawled *Otto Muhlbach.* This may be justifiable, even so it's a little disconcerting.

All right, Otto, here you are. Now since you're working with the U.S. collection would you mind if I looked through the foreign album?

Otto shrugs. Suit yourself.

Muhlbach opens the paperbound Adventurer Album, subtitled *Postage Stamps of the World*, and almost remembers buying it, probably at Woolworth's. In any event it is a much less impressive book than the majestic Scott National. More like a magazine. The paper has dried out, yellowed like an old window shade, and there are only about a hundred pages to accommodate every stamp from Abyssinia to Zululand—which is patently ridiculous. The Maldive Islands, Malta, Mauritius, the Mariannas, the Marshalls, Marienwerder, Memel and Manchukuo, for instance, all are expected to fit on a single page. Well, so be it. Besides, the page is practically blank. Nothing but a couple of uninspired British halfpennies from Malta.

Mauritania, the Middle Congo, Mesopotamia, Modena and Montserrat show some improvement. Three handsome Moyen-Congo stamps representing the Viaduc de Mindouli with a railroad train steaming across. A one-centime desert scene from Mauritanie, Afrique Occidentale Française.

Then all at once Muhlbach remembers Costa Rica—that set of splendidly colored triangles and parallelograms which had cost an entire month's allowance. Quickly he turns back, worried that Otto may have traded them for a dull yellowish brown picture of Warren G. Harding or a faded lilac engraving of the Lincoln memorial. But Otto has not disposed of them. They are exactly where they should be, where they have been for so many years, a bit crooked on the page, clinging by brittle hinges bought sometime during the first ice age from the stamp department of T. O. Cramer's Bookstore.

He looks at them attentively. Here is a commemorative from the Exposición Nacional, Diciembre 1937—a crisp gray-green two-centimos fish, a tuna. And a monoplane, presumably a mail plane, flying not very high above the smoking crater of Volcán Poás. And a coffee-colored three-centimos cacao plant. And an uncut sheet of four futuristic triangular stamps, each a different color, in honor of the Segunda Exposición Filatélica de Costa Rica, which also took place in December of 1937, manifestly an important year. And while contemplating this distinctive issue he begins to remember a wet dark miserable thundering afternoon when he stayed home from school sneezing and coughing, his nose as red as a Christmas tree bulb, when he was ordered to swallow some sort of abominable stinking syrup every two hours.

A bright flag-crossed Ecuadorian series honors the Sesquicentenario de la Adopción y Promulgación de la Constitución de los Estados Unidos de America. These huge gaudy stamps ought to excite a memory so Muhlbach concentrates on them, glaring first at the eagle and next at the condor, determined to pull something from the shadows—anything. But the stamps refuse to cooperate. He remembers them, yet he cannot summon the day he paid for them or traded for them, nor the moment he licked the hinges. That day has been lost.

Estonia. Nothing from Estonia.

Egypt. Five Egyptian stamps in peculiar shades of orange and brown with incomprehensible Arabic lettering, featuring a baby-faced potentate wearing his fez who otherwise is stylishly dressed in the latest European suit. And the sphinx and the principal pyramid in a sickly shade of pink. And a bizarre old mail plane, crudely engraved, coasting ponderously across an engraved desert among engraved clouds.

Elobey, Annobon, and Corisco—Spanish islands in the Gulf of Guinea. No stamps.

Muhlbach turns another page.

The Falklands. Fiji. Fiume. Finland. France has been allotted two pages. Much of the république's space has been filled, mostly with the familiar goddess sowing grain, but there is also a Centenaire Algérie with a face value of fifty centimes, a two-franc Arc de Triomphe, and a mutilated Exposition Internationale. Quite a few bona fide products of France, though none very stimulating. All rather ordinary.

Next comes the French Congo. French Guiana. French Morocco. French Soudan. French India. French Oceania.

At last one escapes the Gallic clutch and comes to Gambia, and then to Georgia, and then to the German colonies, and ultimately to the Fatherland itself where nearly every Deutches Reich issue has been overprinted. Seventy-five tausend marks instead of 400 marks. Two millionen marks. And here are all those rigid Prussian eagles and scythe-swingers and muscular pickaxe-swingers. Not a truly attractive postage stamp in the lot. The Germans of the twenties and thirties must have had other business on their minds.

Then Gibraltar. Then the Gilbert and Ellice Islands in the Pacific—one halfpenny revenue stamp, canceled, for the Crown of England. Great Britain itself, consisting mostly of goateed monarchs in profile. Then Greece and Guadeloupe and Guam and the Grand Comoro Islands—Muhlbach pauses to read the description. Grand Comoro no longer issues stamps, it now belongs to Madagascar.

And so he turns the pages, distracted by these colorful little saw-toothed government vouchers from all over the world. Lambeth has been forgotten. Or, if she swims just below the level of consciousness, not quite forgotten, nevertheless she has been submerged.

Guinea. Horta. Imhambane. Imhambane, which is a port in Mozambique, has gone the way of Grand Comoro—no more stamps. That's too bad. Anybody would like to have a stamp from a place called Imhambane.

Next comes Guatemala.

Muhlbach hesitates, frowning. Guatemala is out of order. Guinea. Horta. Imhambane. Guatemala. Why has the alphabetical sequence been violated? Ah! Yes, it's all in the interest of economy. Horta and Imhambane, being as insignificant as they are, at least in the philatelic sense, have been granted so little space that it seemed advisable to pack them in with Guinea. Guatemala gets most of the next page, followed by Haiti. All right, so much for that. Now what do we have from Guatemala? Well, not a great deal. Christopher Columbus, known as Colón, worth one peso, dressed in his bathrobe, standing heroically on top of an ornate pillar. The Palacio de Minerva, worth diez centavos. And last but not least we have J. Rufino Barrios, whoever he may have been, on horseback. Not merely on horseback, no indeed. He is leading the charge. His noble mount, as valorous as its master, can scarcely wait to leap the trenches. What a magnificent stamp. Maybe the description of Guatemala will tell us about J. Rufino Barrios.

Guatemala exports some five million bunches of bananas per year, together with coffee, chicle, lumber and sugar. Two-thirds of its people are Indians, most of the remainder are mestizos—half-breeds. The natives are poor, the great plantations which provide work for them are owned by a few white people. The national emblem, appearing on many of its postage stamps, is the sacred quetzal bird of the ancient Aztecs, from whom the present inhabitants are descended. That's it. Nothing about the illustrious equestrian.

Muhlbach, after a final glance at Minerva's temple, Columbus and Señor Barrios, moves on to Haiti.

Otto interrupts. He was at Wolfer's last week and saw a Founding of Jamestown plate block with real good centering.

Is that so?

Otto nudges the idea a little further. It was only a hundred and sixty bucks.

That's quite a lot.

Heck, it's a bargain. Usually they cost about a dozen times as much.

You don't say.

Otto goes back to work with his magnifying glass, evidently having concluded that the moment is not propitious. But the Jamestown plate block will pop up again. One balmy Sunday morning, perhaps. Or some evening after the stock market has rallied, during dessert, because Otto should not be underestimated. Even so, one hundred and sixty dollars won't be going down the drain at Wolfer's—not unless he himself has earned it.

Muhlbach returns to Haiti. But for some reason which he cannot quite articulate he finds himself once again looking at the Guatemala stamps. And then gradually he remembers the snowy night on the bus when he saw Lambeth for the first time. He remembers that he had been studying a Guatemala travel brochure.

Now where is the brochure? What's become of it? He tries to recall throwing it away, or putting it someplace, because he is sure it is no longer in his overcoat pocket. Still, it could be.

He shuts the album and after saying goodnight to Otto, and reminding him to get a haircut, he walks down the hall to the closet. He puts his hand into the pocket of his winter coat. The brochure is not there—only some lint and a couple of nickels. Nor is it in any of the other pockets. Possibly Mrs. Grunthe would know something about it. But of course the brochure isn't important.

I suppose I could pick up another one, he thinks while settling himself in his green leather reading chair. As a matter of fact I just might. Not Guatemala necessarily, any place would do. Costa Rica. Bermuda. Martha's Vineyard. Well, my horizon seems to be contracting, but the point is I'd like to get away for a while. I feel exhausted. She took so much out of me, more than I realized. More than I care to admit. Or maybe to some extent it's the heat, this is starting off to be a long summer. I don't know. Whatever the reason, my age perhaps, I feel so tired.

Having unlaced his shoes and unbuttoned the top of his shirt, he slumps in the chair. The house is silent. The TV has been turned off, which means Donna is in bed, and Mrs. Grunthe has stopped clanging around in the kitchen. The leather chair is pleasantly cool. It is easier to sit and meditate than to read or listen to records.

And as he thinks about Lambeth he imagines her diminishing like a figure left at the station when the train pulls out. And he begins to wonder if, wherever she is, she will look back at him the same way. He wonders if she will mimic him for somebody's entertainment—

Jarvis perhaps, or somebody else. Perhaps a group of strangers at another party. The way I stand, the way I talk, and my manners and my expression. She's good at it. Yes, I expect she will. But at least I won't be there. I'd hate to hear them laughing at me—whatever I am.

How did she see me? What did she find in me? I doubt if I'll ever know. Nor will I know what kept us apart. Was I to blame or was she? Or could it have been the two of us? And although it's over it seems incomplete. Our relationship was like a seed that lay on the ground but never sprouted.

THE next afternoon, muggy and overcast, threatening rain, Muhlbach is at his desk studying a report on the possibility of arson at a chemical plant in Springfield when the intercom light winks on and Gloria informs him that Dr. O'Reilly is calling.

Who? I don't know any Dr. O'Reilly. Did he say what he wanted?

He said he's got to talk to you. I'll tell him you're in conference.

No, wait. Put him through.

I can dump him. I'll say you're gone for the day.

Put him through, Gloria. I'll take the call.

And a moment later he hears the earnest young Midwestern voice:

Mr. Muhlbach? This is Jarvis O'Reilly. Do you remember me?

Muhlbach finds that he cannot speak; his throat, for some inexplicable reason, feels as stiff as a reed. Then to his astonishment he notices that his free hand—which had been resting comfortably on the blotter—has curled up into a fist. He takes a deep deliberate breath.

Yes. Yes, he repeats. Yes, Dr. O'Reilly, I know who you are.

I wasn't sure because we only met for a minute outside that delicatessen.

I remember you. Go on.

Okay. I'm sorry to interrupt. I know you're busy. But I thought I should tell you something. I don't know exactly how to begin. I guess I should have called sooner. Anyway, here's the situation. Lambeth either jumped or fell from her apartment and she's at Roosevelt Hospital in critical condition. She was in a coma until just a little while ago.

Are you there now?

Yes, sir. I got here not long after she jumped. A buddy of mine happened to be on duty and he notified me.

I'll get there as soon as possible.

Okay. I'll meet you at the reception desk.

When did this happen?

About five o'clock.

This morning? Five o'clock this morning?

Yes, sir. Like I said, maybe I should have called sooner. I thought about that. I probably should have.

All right, never mind, Muhlbach answers sharply. Is she expected to survive?

She's got a chance.

I'll leave at once.

After having told Gloria that he will be gone for an indefinite period he hurries to the closet for his raincoat and umbrella. Five this morning! he thinks. And the knowledge that he had spent the day as usual while she was lying close to death—this seems to him grotesque.

How could she have fallen? he asks himself again and again. Unless she was pushed. That boy first said she 'jumped or fell,' then he changed his story and said 'jumped.' Maybe she was pushed.

Arriving at the hospital he shuts his umbrella, slaps the moisture from it and strides toward the reception area.

Jarvis—helmet haircut, turtleneck, tinted glasses, plaid pants and all—Jarvis is waiting, leaning confidentially against the desk chatting with a plump young nurse, a bottle of Pepsi-Cola in his beefy hand.

Muhlbach makes no attempt to disguise his anger. Where can we talk without being overheard? he demands, gripping the umbrella like a sword.

Jarvis, instead of answering, takes a long swallow of Pepsi-Cola. Then he straightens up and leads the way. Muhlbach follows.

Has there been any change in her condition?

Jarvis wags his head. Nope.

You told me she might pull through.

Yep.

Do you know the physician in charge?

Yep. Andy Price. He's a good man.

Do you know exactly what's wrong with her?

Well, yes and no. The left side of her body is paralyzed and there's subarcnoid bleeding. We don't know the extent of her internal injuries.

What does 'subarcnoid bleeding' indicate?

Brain damage, Jarvis replies after another swallow of Pepsi-Cola.

Muhlbach, enraged, tries to control himself. All right, suppose you tell me how this happened.

I wasn't there.

You said she 'jumped.'

Jarvis shrugs. I don't know if it was an accident or she decided to kill herself. Oh hell, yes I do.

But if you were not there how do you know?

Look, Jarvis continues while rolling the bottle between his palms, I wasn't under any obligation to call you. Now I wish I hadn't.

Perhaps I owe you an apology, says Muhlbach with an effort. I'm afraid I may have sounded more critical than I had any right to.

That's okay. Suppose we forget it.

I knew when I spoke to her last night that she was extremely distraught but—forgive me, I seem to be babbling.

No need to apologize.

This is such a jolt. I can't believe it.

Well, I can believe it. But you didn't know her like I did. The fact is, she used to flip out every once in a while. She'd be practically normal for weeks or even months, just excitable and high-strung, you know, like she was, but then without any warning she'd come unglued. Scream. Break stuff. Tear up whatever got in her path. She never did that with you?

No.

You're lucky. It was no picnic. I guess she respected you too much. She didn't want to let it all hang out. She didn't respect very many people that I know of. Anyhow I sure wasn't one of them. You should've heard the names she called me. Oh, brother! It's good I got a tough hide. That's what my old man taught me. He said, 'Jarv, you're gonna get clobbered but never let 'em know it hurts.' If I wasn't tough she'd have done me in.

Jarvis drops the empty bottle into a wastebasket, hitches up his pants and resumes talking:

Well, so then she'd come out of it and seem to be all right. But man, did those fits spook me. Once she ripped off her clothes and climbed out on the fire escape. Another time I caught her in the bathtub with a razor—sitting there like a zombie. Wow. I used to think maybe she'd loosen up and confide in me but finally I said to myself nope, she can't. No way. She was walled in. That must be awful. I mean, to face a brick wall wherever you turn.

Are you convinced she jumped?

I know she did.

Couldn't it have been accidental?

I doubt it. I tried to tell myself she got bombed and leaned out the window for a breath of air—because I've seen her falling down drunk. It was unbelievable, a woman as beautiful as that too drunk to stand up. But anyhow, she didn't fall.

How can you be sure?

I feel it. I just feel it.

Will she recover?

Jarvis, after scratching his head, peers at something far away. Mr. Muhlbach, you mentioned owing me an apology but the fact is I owe you one.

For what?

I should have told you as soon as you got here but there were all those people around. In fact I should have told you on the phone, but I couldn't force myself to.

Speak up. What is it?

She's dead.

She is what?

I couldn't figure out the best time to break the news. I kept asking myself when would be the best time. Over the phone, or as soon as you got here, or after we'd talked for a while. But there wasn't any best time.

You say Lambeth is dead?

Yes, sir. She died twenty or thirty minutes ago. I don't know how long it's been, I'm so bushed I can hardly see straight. She died just before I called you. Hey listen, this might sound peculiar but would you mind going to the cafeteria?

The cafeteria?

Muhlbach stares at him.

Jarvis shrugs. Can I help it if I'm hungry?

I know it sounds crazy but I haven't had anything to eat since last night and I'm starving. Really starving. I mean, unless you've got to leave.

In the cafeteria, blinking with the effort to stay awake, he splatters catsup on a hamburger, takes a bite, and after wiping his mouth on a paper napkin he continues:

I lost count of how many times today I've asked myself why. Why? Why? Because I thought she was happy with me. Not happy like most people. That wasn't in the cards for her. But—oh, I don't know. I'm so groggy I'm out of my skull.

Let me ask you something. She mentioned while we were in Connecticut that an attempt had been made on her life. Was there any truth in it?

Jarvis smiles thinly. I knew somebody had to be with her. I couldn't figure out where she went but I knew she'd never take off for the weekend alone.

I assumed she had told you.

No, but it doesn't matter. Anyway, about the question, all I can tell you is that when we were living together I came home one night and found her beaten half to death—like she'd been worked over with a pool cue. Her face was swollen up like a melon. It was awful. There was blood on the floor and in the bathroom. I couldn't get near her. She screamed every time I touched her. I've seen some pretty bad cases in emergency but not many in worse shape than she was. I was afraid they'd messed her up internally. She never did tell me who did it or why, but it had to be a warning. I mean, whoever it was could have finished her off.

Jarvis pauses for a little while, chewing thoughtfully.

Sometimes she'd get a call in the middle of the night. She'd get dressed and leave without a word. It scared the piss out of me. I tried to get her to stop whatever she was doing but she told me to mind my own business. They didn't come back for her last night though, she did it to herself. She'd tried it before.

Suicide?

Didn't you notice her wrists?

What do you mean?

The scars.

No. No, I didn't.

That's funny, I thought you would. From what she told me about you I figured you noticed little details like that. Anyway that's how I met her. They carted her into St. Vincent's while I was interning there. And if she had a teacup of blood left in her body you couldn't tell from looking.

In other words she owed her life to you.

Nope. I had this buddy on duty who told me to stop by if I wanted to see something spectacular. I'd never seen a woman like that, just in magazines or on the stage. It was—well, she was too much. I looked at her and I could hardly move. Really, I felt—I can't explain.

Did you love her?

I guess I did. I wanted to marry her.

Because of her appearance?

It was more than that. I liked her. I liked her even after I realized how buggy she was. I still think maybe if we'd had a chance to get started, to get organized—I mean if we could have gotten out of New York. You wouldn't believe how I hate this place! The crap. The corruption. We could have made it, I think. I could have brought her around to some kind of normalcy, enough so she could keep going. If we had just had time. If we could have gotten out of here. I wanted to set up practice in Jefferson City, which is where I'm from. Maybe she told you. I know of a house for sale three blocks from where my sister lives and that's where I want to live. So Lambeth would say great one day but the next day act like she never heard of it. She'd have enjoyed it, though, once she got used to being there. She was a terrible cook and didn't know how to sew. Hell, she had trouble sewing buttons. One night she tried to bake a chocolate pie for me as a surprise—using that prepared stuff where all you do is read the directions—and it was pathetic. I could have baked a better pie myself. She couldn't do anything—that's what was so sad. Nothing except those little tissue-paper pictures. And she was pretty good at imitating people. She liked to do that. I had a feeling if she'd gotten serious about it she might have been able to do that professionally, but she could never focus on anything very long. She never could finish what she started. I don't know why. And she never actually seemed to enjoy anything. Didn't like sports. Wouldn't go to a ball game with me. Didn't care about politics, didn't even know who was running. Didn't want to go out camping. I enjoy that—camping out. It's great. The woods and all. Nope, not Lambeth. Diddle around this rotten filthy city, that was it. Well anyhow, I thought once we started raising a family she couldn't afford to spend all day acting neurotic. Shoot, not with a house full of kids and the laundry and so forth. That was what she needed—something to do. Are you married, by the way?

I was.

Any kids?

Two.

How do you get along with them?

Despite the eruptions I would say fairly well.

I dig kids. The whole family scene, I really dig that. You watch your kids grow up while you and your wife grow old together. It's beautiful. Have you got boys or girls?

One apiece.

What's your son's name?

He was named for his grandfather. Otto.

What does he want to be?

He can't make up his mind.

Does he like to fish?

Oh yes. Yes indeed. Although the opportunities are rather limited, living in the city.

I used to go fishing with my uncle. My father, too, at first. Dad was a Rock Island brakeman. He was killed two weeks before my twelfth birthday. I don't know exactly how. Nobody at the terminal saw it happen but they said he must have slipped. It was January and there was a lot of new snow on the tracks, so probably he did slip. Anyhow, after he died I had to pretend all the stuff we'd do together—camping out and hunting and, oh, you know what I mean. My uncle tried real hard to fill in, but mostly he just liked to shoot pool or play cards. Fishing, he said, why go to all that trouble when you can get it at the market? Well, excuse me for talking so much. But I sure envy you, Mr. Muhlbach.

You envy me? May I ask why?

You're mature and successful and you've got the scene under control. I'm so fucked up—excuse the expression. But I really am, especially now with Lambeth gone—just when I was beginning to think I could pull it together. Pretty soon I'll be finished here. We could have gotten married and moved to the Midwest. Now I don't know. I'm not sure what to do. I hate this place.

Jarvis sits motionless, looking into his half-finished bowl of soup with distaste as though he had discovered a bug or a strand of hair.

I never did understand your relationship with her. I didn't know if she meant something to you or if she was just somebody you could use. She was being used all the time. Everybody figured that was okay. Use her. Jimmy Frye, the bastard! Listen, I'm sorry, Mr. Muhlbach, I don't know what I'm saying. I'm out on my feet. Wow, am I ready for bed.

Who is Jimmy Frye?

A pop singer. A black dude. He got an overdose of smack a couple of months ago. It was in the papers.

What's smack?

Heroin.

How does this concern Lambeth?

He'd send for her. Just whenever he felt the urge. She'd get a message saying meet him at such and such a hotel where he had a gig. It turned my stomach. She'd drop everything and split. Chicago. Detroit. Louisville. No matter where he was, she went. The first time that happened I felt like killing her but after a while I sort of got used to it. I didn't have much choice. She told me to get lost if I couldn't handle it.

Was she in love with him?

She told me he made her feel special. Like a queen, she said. 'He makes me feel like a queen.' I couldn't believe my ears. Anyway, whenever he sent for her, off she went. So I guess she was in love with him. It's funny, isn't it? She could have had her pick. You know how it was—just walking along the street with her—people turning around to look. So what did she pick? A black junkie.

Did you meet him?

Nope. I'd have wrung his neck. Or maybe on second thought I'd have asked him how to deal with her.

Did you meet a little Central American by the name of Rafael López y Fuentes?

That creep. He was always after her. I never saw such a persistent little creep. She couldn't stand him. I mean, really! She went out with him a few times because he paid her. It was a big ego trip for him. Once when he came by to pick her up I was in my pajamas—I'd just got off duty and was going to take a nap—and you should have seen his face.

How about Veach?

Who's Veach?

Nobody. Another one, that's all.

She was something, wasn't she?

And then, rubbing his face and yawning, Jarvis goes on:

I knew it had to happen sooner or later. I used to tell myself all we needed was to get out of New York. If we could get out of here and make it back home where at least you can take a walk in the evening without worrying about a knife in the ribs or running into some degenerate creep—that's what I used to tell myself. But of course it isn't that simple. It's more than this lousy city. There was something about Lambeth herself. I mean, like she knew she was never going to make it. Like she knew what cards were about to turn up. Some people know, I think. And she knew. I could just sense it. So I've been sort of expecting this. I'm relieved, in a way. I shouldn't say that, but it's a fact.

Well, Muhlbach remarks after a long silence, perhaps it's time for me to go. Unless there's something I can do.

No. There's nothing.

Has her mother been here?

Nope.

Why not?

They can't locate her. She's probably drunk, passed out someplace.

What about her sister?

Nope. I think Judy moved, but I don't know where. And she had a kid brother named Mickey who's supposed to be in military school but I think he took off and joined a rock music band.

And her father is dead?

Yep, he had a coronary five or six years ago.

So she was alone. Except for an alcoholic mother.

Uh huh, says Jarvis, yawning. Not even any girl friends, which is no surprise. Only this line of studs waiting to climb on like she was a carousel at an amusement park.

Did she talk to you about a Swedish ship owner named Axel Svensen?

Sometimes. When she was bombed out of her skull.

And the dancer Erica Branch?

Her 'mother'—who would have been famous if she hadn't died a tragic death in Luxembourg. Yeah, sure.

What sense could you make of it?

None.

Did she ever meet Svensen?

I couldn't tell you, Mr. Muhlbach. I had the feeling she did. I have a hunch she knew him, but maybe not. She was so full of crazy dreams. I gave up asking questions, trying to separate the dreams from the reality. You might as well try to separate the bird from the egg. So I'd just say okay, sure Lambeth, okay. That was the best solution.

Perhaps it was, Muhlbach thinks. Who knows? Because I don't. And then, a bit stiff in the joints from the rigid cafeteria chair, he leans forward and with an effort boosts himself to his feet.

Jarvis, after a quick spoonful of soup, also gets up.

It's not likely we'll see each other again.

Probably not.

Can I be of help to you in any way?

No. I'll get it together. Do you want me to walk to the front door with you?

That isn't necessary.

Okay, I guess I'll stay here a while. I could use another bowl of soup. Incidentally, she asked for you.

For me?

At the very end she kept saying 'I want Karl.' She must have said it three or four times. I'd have called you—after I figured out who she meant—except it was too late.

She had promised me a collage, Muhlbach answers. But the remark sounds inappropriate.

Jarvis yawns again. Sorry! You mean those little paper things?

Yes.

I never could see the point of them. What a waste of time.

Muhlbach, unable to think of a suitable comment, begins to button his raincoat.

Jarvis, blinking, watches attentively.

At last the coat is buttoned.

Muhlbach holds out his hand. Good-bye, Jarvis.

So long, Mr. Muhlbach. It's lucky you brought your umbrella. Sounds like it's starting to rain pretty hard.

Yes. Yes, so it does. Well, I appreciate your notifying me.

Sure. No trouble.

And the rain is indeed coming down. Just inside the entrance Muhlbach pauses, leaning on his umbrella, listening to the occasional distant boom of thunder while he contemplates the activity on the street, and it seems to him that he may have been partly responsible for Lambeth's death. One word might have been enough to change the course of her life, if only he had spoken it.

Yet what was the word?

Unless, that is, she didn't jump or fall. Despite what Jarvis thought, she could have been murdered. The boy had no proof, simply an opinion or an intuition. As a matter of fact there was some evidence indicating the possibility of murder. That time she was beaten. Those mysterious instructions in the middle of the night. And apparently she was involved with a vicious cop. How many other malevolent savage people was she involved with? And for what purposes? And why?

Well, he thinks, I don't know and perhaps I'll never know. It's conceivable that she was murdered—thrown from a window. But I'm no detective. If in fact she was murdered it may come out. Angelo whatever his name is—he'll be checking into the possibility. Although he himself might have killed her, from what Veach said. On the other hand maybe Jarvis was right. Why do I keep suggesting to myself that she was murdered?

He peers through the glass door, shaking his head in slow amazement at the traffic on the street and the people hurrying in all directions. Everything goes on as usual, as though this day were no different.

Thunder rattles and explodes above the hospital. The rain slants down still more furiously. The door opens and shuts, briefly letting in the sound of the rain splashing against the concrete. Visitors arrive and depart. All over New York the rain must be falling like this—falling everywhere, equally and insistently on office buildings and apartments, in Harlem as well as on Fifth Avenue brownstones, on the docks, in the Village, soaking everybody who happens to be outside—flowing through the gutters, collecting in pools on deserted rooftops and in silent playgro

tradesmen and schoolchildren and police and messengers on bicycles and newspaper vendors and women scurrying between shops.

It occurs to him that all of these people obsessed by their insignificant affairs in the diagonal rain look like figures from a Japanese woodcut. Lifting his head he squints at the ragged greenish sky and reflects that there is not much point in standing around. The rain doesn't intend to let up. Still, it seems wrong to leave. There's no reason to remain but it seems wrong to leave. I suppose I'm acting squeamish, he says to himself. There's absolutely nothing I can do. Nothing. Tomorrow and tomorrow and tomorrow and there's nothing I can do. Maybe I could have brought her out of it, if only we'd gotten better acquainted. But everything happened so fast. It was like being dropped in the eye of a hurricane. Or seeing the storm from a distance—I don't know. All I know is that I didn't understand her. I could just as easily read the hieroglyphics on those baked clay tablets in museums. Well, I must go. I have things to do.

So, having spread his umbrella and turned up his collar, Muhlbach steps outside to join the crowd. And presently, if seen from a distance, he could not be distinguished from the rest.